THE CELL BLOCK PRESENTS...

MOB TALES

Published by: THE CELL BLOCK™

THE CELL BLOCK
P.O. Box 1025
Rancho Cordova, CA 95741

Website: thecellblock.net
Facebook/thecellblockofficial
Instagram: @mikeenemigo

Copyright© The Cell Block

Cover design by Mike Enemigo

Send comments, reviews, or other business
inquiries: info@thecellblock.net

DEVILS &
DEMONS
The Prequel

CHAPTER ONE

DEMONS IN THE MIDST

"Blood, look! Baby got a burner!"
– Talton

The box of greasy Church's Chicken tasted like gourmet food to the trio of goonies parked underneath the shade tree on 4th Avenue. Talton, Terauchi and Kenyata were in Talton's scraper devouring their fried chicken and okras.

All three of them were cousins. Talton was the oldest, at 18. Kenyata was a year younger. Terauchi was 14. They were from a neighborhood in Sacramento called Oak Park. Their section was also known as the "Murder Mids" since it sat in the center of the city and was the breeding ground for some of the city's most notorious criminals.

It was an especially dangerous time in the city of Sacramento. Part of the reason was directly connected to the recent wave of releases from CYA and CDC of known criminals who had earned their parole. Talton, along with several other factors from his 'hood were part of that wave of parolees.

4th Avenue and San Jose Way was a known cut in the "P." Talton had a drug house that he trapped out of less than half a football field away from where they were currently squelching their munchies. It was where he sold double-ups to younger dealers who bled the block for their kibbles and bits. The long-haired gangsta was as dangerous as they came. Yet, getting money was his highest motivating factor.

Kenyata wasn't just his cousin. Kenya was his ace! Their swagger was identical to each other's. It was a common occurrence for them to get mistaken for twins. Although he kept a lower profile on the streets, the people closest to them could safely argue that Kenyata was more of a hothead than his older cousin. Individually, they were a problem for their opps. But, together they were a force.

Terauchi was the youngest of the young gunners. At 14, he was less experienced but just as ferocious. Which was inevitable since he was raised by the same streets that molded career criminals. He knew he was getting on his older cousin's nerves that afternoon but he didn't care. He wasn't trying to let go of a conversation that should have ended hours earlier.

"You know you wrong, right?" Terauchi said between bites.

Talton sighed before wiping his mouth with a napkin and saying, "You too young, 'Rauchi. I don't know how many times I gotta tell you this."

"Stop crying," Kenya told Terauchi. "You'll be off the bench soon enough. And trust when I say this; when your name is finally called, you're gonna be sicker than half the niggaz out here."

"Anyways," Talton started. "After we pass, we all finna be up!"

"That's right," Kenya agreed. "On Bloods, I got you, relly. Just bick back. It'll be good in the end." Terauchi shook his head and continued eating. He knew nothing he said would get him a ticket on their current money train. That didn't matter though. He would keep trying until they finally did let him in on a lick of that caliber.

$$$$$

J-Bone was on one that morning. He woke up with eighteen dollars in his pocket and was dead set on getting high twice with that money. For the last week, he had been smoking dope on a daily basis. It was surprising how much he was able to scrape by with all his small-time cons. His daily routine revolved around getting high on his drug of choice. Filling his pipe with hard white was all that mattered to him. And so far, ever since he was released from prison, he managed to stay on cloud crack.

When he hit the Ave that day, his mission was simple: to get more drugs than he was willing to pay for. This wasn't really hard for him. He picked up his drug addiction while in prison and during that time he picked up enough tactics to allow him to run circles around the average corner hustler. The young ones who barely stepped off the porch were his favorite marks. They were easily manipulated. When that didn't work, he usually regressed to an intimidation tactic. That route always worked, especially since his prison term gave him a chiseled frame.

J-Bone didn't have to wait too long after arriving to the spot before he found a victim. The Ave was a gold mine when it came to finding block bleeders. Drugs were everywhere.

Mm-hmmm, he thought to himself when he saw a young Spanish-looking female on the block. She didn't look like she was there for anything in particular so she had to be grinding, he assured himself. *But, for who?* he asked himself as he scanned the block. There were a few Parksters who had their females hustling for them but not many. Since he hadn't seen her before he naturally assumed she was out there alone. That was a dangerous thing to be doing and he was about to be the man to show her why, he told himself before peddling up to her on his mountain bike and asked, "You working?"

"Yeah," she replied. "What's up?" Jomara was a 17-year-old juvenile delinquent with an attitude problem. She was fairly new to the 'hood, but not *too* new.

J-Bone got off his bike and nonchalantly laid it on the curb before approaching her. Every move was calculated. He was quickly deciding to go with an intimidation tactic. If that didn't work, knocking her out then going through her pockets was most definitely an option.

"Gimme something for thirty!" he demanded roughly.

"Let me see the bread!" she replied just as aggressively.

J-Bone gave her a better look and thought, *Okay... The little bitch got 'hood in 'er*. Out loud he said, "What? You think I'm finna rob you for them punk-ass crumbs? Don't be scared, lil mamma."

"My name's Jomara, homey. You want this shit, or not?"

Bone laughed to himself. Knocking her out was going to be a pleasure. He took a crumpled stack of bills out of his dirty jeans and made the exchange. Without waiting for her to count the money he turned around and grabbed his bike.

"Hey!" Jomara barked. "This ain't thirty!"

"So what, bitch!"

"What!? Gimme my money!"

"Bitch, who you raising your voice at? You got me fucked up!" J-Bone slowly laid his bike back down onto the curb. She was feeding right into his plan. It was looking to him like he was gonna come up nice and quick this afternoon.

"Fuck dat!" she spat, not showing any fear whatsoever. "Gimme my money, or the work! Now!"

"You got me fucked up!" J-Bone said while slowly approaching her.

Jomara knew what came next. She had her nigga-get-off-me tool at the small of her back and she wasn't planning on leaving it there for long. "Naw, nigga! You got *me* fucked up!"

J-Bone didn't even realize she was reaching. His cockiness only allowed him to see from point A to point B: knocking her out then going through her pockets, bra, or panties for her stash of pebbles and change.

In Jomara's head she was already mapping out in which direction she was going to run after shooting him in the face. One thing she couldn't stand was a bully. She felt as if she had been through way too much in her short time on this earth to allow a crackhead to punk her in any way. She held her ground as she slowly pulled her heater from the small of her back...

$$$$$

Terauchi was the first one to see what was going on up the street. "Check out J-Bone! That nigga finna do something to that Mexican bitch."

Kenya looked at the scene and asked, "Who is that?"

"I don't know," Talton replied. "I never seen her before."

Kenyata took a better look then said, "I know her! That's one of Nikki's friends. She just moved out here 'bout six months ago. She from New York or something."

"Blood, look at 'er!" Talton remarked. Baby got a burner! She finna blast blood!"

"On da B!" Terauchi agreed.

Talton turned the ignition on and quickly put the car in gear.

From the passenger seat, Kenya asked, "Whatchu doin', blood?"

"We can't let 'er shoot J-Bone, blood. The pigs'll be on the block nonstop for the next week! We don't need that type of heat out here. It's already hot as fuck!"

Talton sped up the half block to where the Spanish girl was arguing with J-Bone. He pulled up to the curb, put the scraper in park and hoped out. The pistol was out, but Bone hadn't seen it yet. Talton had barely made it in time.

"Hey! Hey!" Talton barked. "What's the problem, Bone?"

"This bitch playin' wit' me!"

"What!?" Jomara started before Talton lightly moved her out the way and stepped between the two. She was about to say something to the light-skinned nigga with the ponytail, but instead stayed quiet. There was something in the way the smoker was looking at him that made her sit back and watch for a second.

By then, Kenya and Terauchi had gotten out the car and took their place next to Talton. It didn't matter that J-Bone banged the 'hood. It was obvious where their allegiance laid.

Talton turned to Jomara and asked, "What's going on, ma?"

For a moment, she stayed stitch-lipped, debating whether she should state her case to these random niggaz. But after quickly assessing the scene, she went with her gut and said, "This nigga asked for a thirty-piece then gave me twelve dollars!

I ain't goin' for dat shit!"

Talton studied the girl's mannerisms. She wasn't scared and that made her even sexier than her extra-large breast and juicy hips did. After checking her out for a little longer than necessary he turned to J-Bone and said, "Give her the work back!"

"Blood!" he pleaded.

"Blood-nothing!" Kenyata hissed from the side. "You heard the homey!"

J-Bone knew not to play with them niggaz. Everyone knew about Talton and his Fourth Avenue clique. They were really about everything the streets offered. From money to murder, they were activated.

Bone addressed Talton, "She got my money."

"Where her work at?" Talton asked, ignoring his statement.

"Right here."

"Give it to 'er!"

7

J-Bone looked from Talton back to the bitch then back at Talton. The whole time, Kenya and Terauchi were in his peripheral looking like hyenas. He handed the rocks back to the girl then looked at Talton.

"Get off the Ave, blood!" Talton ordered. "You got a pass this time. But, on Bloods, nigga. You come over here again wit' that bullshit and you ain't making IT home."

J-Bone grabbed his mountain bike and took off.

As soon as he left, Kenya and Terauchi went back to their Church's Chicken meals. Talton looked at the girl and extended his hand, "I'm Gangsta."

"My name's Jomara."

"Where you from, ma?"

Jomara held his gaze. She enjoyed looking at him. His gold chain sparkled from its spot on his brand-new black T. His crispy grey jeans and fresh Jordans were on point too. "I'm from the island."

"What island?"

"P.R."

He smiled. She was sexy. "Puerto Rico, huh? And you be grinding? You're a unique one."

"I just do me, ya' know?"

"Yeah. I feel you. Look, if you ever need some work, I got you. That house over there with the tree in the yard is my spot."

"What? You got double-ups?"

"Yeah."

"A'ight. I might fuck wit'chu."

Her eyes held Talton's in place. Words weren't necessary, there was an obvious spark between them.

"Blood! We gotta go," Kenya called out from the car.

8

Talton nodded at him before turning back towards her and saying, "Alright, Jomara. I'll see you in traffic."

"Maybe..."

CHAPTER TWO

OAK PARK MARK

"There's gonna come a time when you're gonna be expected to drive the car yourself..."
– Talton

Mark Sanders was a gangland prodigy. Not only was he also from Oak Park, he actually helped mold the foundation in which made it a Damu neighborhood. He was fresh out of prison on a mission to reestablish himself as a factor within the city's underworld. M.S. was a heavyweight who stood six feet, four inches. Even if he hadn't been as big as he was, his sociopathic character would've kept the hounds at bay. Which was actually a good thing where he grew up at.

Although M.S. was known for getting money, he still lived with his grandmother on 12th Avenue behind Oak Park Market. His granny raised him his whole life, so whenever he came home from doing time, he always went back to live with her. Years later, he would inherit the home along with others.

Oak Park Mark would have been classified as a serial killer if the Feds ever got a whiff of his confirmed kills. His whole family was from the P. The Park was all he knew. As a young teen he ran with an older crowd, not only because of his size, but also since he came from a large family. Yet, as he grew into the man he was destined to become, he picked up the traits of a teacher. That was part of the reason his inner circle usually consisted of younger demons.

On this particular afternoon the vibe was all business. His living room was being used as a think-tank where he was brainstorming with two of his partnas. Insane B and Joe Blood both banged 12th Avenue but that didn't matter on most days. Oak Park was Oak Park. Circles within circles were constantly created to protect one from the other.

Mark sat down on the Lay-Z-Boy next to the coffee table and leaned in to address his dogs. "Lettie said her manager is outta town for the next week. He'll be gone, but –"

"But what?" Joe Blood asked. His eyes were bloodshot from the weed he was passing around the table.

"She said her manager's wife was running things. Mrs. Browning. We all know that bitch and how she is."

"She's a hawk!" Insane B interjected.

"She might be," Mark continued. "But none of that shit matters when there's a legion of killas pointing guns in her face. I'm sure we can count on her to do as she's told. Feel me?"

"Yeah. Damn right!" Joe Blood agreed. "But, blood. Why it gotta be on Sunday night? Wouldn't there be more money in that bitch after it closes on Friday or Saturday?"

Mark took a long look at his homey. Joe Blood was a mature 17-year-old with heart. But he still had a lot to learn. "Pizza places hold on to all their money until they can deposit it all into the bank. Since most banks close

11

early on Saturdays, restaurants and bars and shit like that be holding on to their money all weekend. They usually take all that shit to the bank on Monday mornings. So, Sundays are the best time to hit shit 'cause –"

"They holding all they bread!" Joe Blood said.

"Onda B!" Mark replied. Then, right before he could say anything else there was a knock at the door. "That should be blood and them right there. Insane, get the door, blood."

$$$$$

Talton wasn't trying to hide the fact that he was standing there watching Jomara walk away. She didn't sway away with an extra switch in her hips like most females would have when they knew they were being watched. Jomara pushed off like she had somewhere to be. In his eyes, she was killing the game. She held herself like one of the homegirls who was sexy as fuck, yet demanded their respect. He liked that.

"Blood!" Kenya yelled from the car. "We gotta go!"

Gangsta snapped back to business. He went back to the Buick and pulled away from the curb. Before their lunches were interrupted the trio were on a set schedule. It was time to get back on course.

Talton bent a few corners until he hit 2nd Avenue. They were heading to their grandmother's house. The green and white house on the Duece was the most secure entity in all three of the teens' lives. It was a place where they could always count on having a comfortable bed and warm plate of food waiting for them. It was also a dependable spot to stash their felonies at. It didn't matter how long they were gone; if any of them ever left anything at their granny's house, they could count on it being there when they came back to get it.

When they got there, Talton told Kenya to go get the duffle bag that was stashed in the shed behind her house. After he left, he looked at Terauchi through the rearview mirror. It wasn't like 'Rauchi was sulking but it was still obvious he was upset about not being included in their upcoming jux. "Rauchi."

"Yeah."

"I know you feeling some type of way 'bout what's going on. I get it, but you really shouldn't even worry about it. Everybody already talked about it and nigga's gonna break bread with you regardless. On some G shit, what's more important is the fact that you're able to sit back and watch everything play out from the cuts. You're really getting laced up on some real Game. You might not realize it now, but this is shit you'll be able to use in the future. There's gonna come a time when you're gonna be expected to drive the car yourself. Experiences like these are gonna have you laced up super tight —"

"I can drive the car now!"

"I bet you could. But you still got more to soak up. Either way, there's always a next time. Trust that!"

When Kenyata came back, he was carrying a large green duffle bag. Talton pressed the trunk's release button and the bag was deposited into it. After that they went on their way. They slithered through side streets trying to dodge the police. The pigs that patrolled the P were aggressive. Racial profiling was the norm. It was part of their protocol. Part of life in the ghetto...

It didn't take long for them to pull up to a house they had been to hundreds of times throughout their lives. After taking the duffle bag out the trunk, they all went up to the front door and waited after Talton knocked. As soon as the door was answered, Talton was greeted with a hearty gangsta's embrace.

"What's brackin', blood!?" Insane B exclaimed. "C'mon in, we been waiting on y'all!"

Mark embraced his best friend, Talton. At 5' 6", Talton was way shorter than his dog but just as dangerous. They all shared a common bond which was their cache of Park experiences. It was the soil they were all enriched from, a dirty soil that couldn't be duplicated purposely.

It didn't take them long to crowd around the coffee table where Kenyata was unceremoniously emptying the duffle bag on. "Damn, Gangsta!" Mark commented after picking up an old Tek 9. I can't believe you still got this bitch!"

"Yup! It was tucked the whole time we was down."

The others each grabbed different guns. There were six firearms in all. A street sweeper, different handguns, a Mac 10 and a Glock.

"Y'all don't even know how dirty these guns is!" Mark bragged. "That .45 been passed down at least two generations, huh, Gangsta?"

"On Bloods!" Talton affirmed. "It's another reason why we can't get caught hitting this pizza place. So, what's brackin'? What's the plan, y'all?"

CHAPTER THREE

DEMONS ON THE STRIP

"I'm on the same shit you be on..."

— Jomara

Sunday nights in Sacramento are always lit. The warm spring evening had the whole city up and moving. Sunday nights on Broadway looked just like Crenshaw. Everyone with a shiny whip was out flossing. And even if they didn't have a car, they were still in attendance looking for something (or someone) to get into.

Jomara was part of that movement too. She was out and about, painting the town in a rented Yukon with her homegirls. Jomara pushed with a squad from the Park who had adopted her as one of their own ever since she enrolled into Sac High as a senior that year. Her "fuck you" attitude along with the "I'ma get mines" mentality caught the attention of a certain crowd of likeminded females, and she quickly got in where she fit in.

Niki, Big Blood and T.P. were well-known P babies. They weren't treated like thots, like other females from the 'hood. They were respected mainly because they respected themselves.

Niki was a dark-skinned beauty known for her hustling skills. She was a jack-of-all-trades. It didn't matter if it was selling crack, boosting clothes, or sliding stolen credit cards, she was with the activities one hundred percent.

Big Blood was a gangsta. She was a thick, Megan-Thee-Stallion type who had hands and liked to fight. She was loyal to a fault and repped the Murder Mids to the fullest.

Tosha Powell was the youngest of the bunch. She was like the little sister of the crew. Cute with a soft voice, but just as with the activities as the rest of them.

The cabin of the SUV was hotboxed while they bent corners through the 'hood that night. All of them were dancing and having fun with the sound system up as loud as it went. Niki was taking them to the designated hangout spot, which was the Taco Bell on Broadway, when she decided to inquire about a subject they had all been wondering about. She turned to look at Jomara in the second row and asked, "Gurrrl, you was on one the other night at Lili's house party. You fuck that nigga Derrick, or what?"

Suddenly, all eyes were on the Puerto Rican girl. They all waited for the answer while assuming the worst. Jomara smiled a teasing, mocking smile before saying, "No! I told y'all already. Derrick cool, but naw. He gave me a ride home, that's it."

"Bitch, you lying!" teased Big Blood.

"No, she ain't," commented T.P. "She likes Gangsta."

Jomara's neck snapped when she turned to look at Tosha; "I never said that!"

"You didn't have to," Niki joked. "You told us all we needed to know once you started asking all them god-damn questions 'bout the homey!"

"I was just checkin' to see if he was good business or not. That's all."

"Umm-hmmm, bitch," Big Blood said sarcastically. "Well, either way I guess it don't matter."

"Why?" Jomara asked.

"'Cause you finna get a chance to fact-check everything we said in a few minutes."

"What'chu talkin' 'bout, bitch?" Jomara asked, a little confused.

Niki saw what Big Blood was talking about and started laughing. "She talking 'bout you talking to Talton. He right there!"

The SUV pulled into the crowded Taco Bell parking lot. Talton had been standing in a crowd towards the middle of the lot. It looked like a sea of red and burgundy. Park gang was everywhere. Their cars were parked close to one another, with their trunks open, blasting their music. The sideshow was lit.

They pulled in slowly, letting all the people (most of them holding red cups) open the way for them. All of them felt the glow. It was all love since they were all recognizable P babies. Niki chose a spot towards the back to park and they all got out. One of them opened the back of the SUV and they started their own tailgate party.

Jomara felt comfortable in her surroundings. She only lived in Sac for a little over six months and already made it her home. She recognized most of the people out there from school, or around the neighborhood. Nevertheless, she still found herself looking around nervously. She searched the crowd for Talton and immediately felt a rush when she laid eyes on him. The sexual attraction was magnetic; at least that's what she felt on her end, she thought to herself.

"There he go," Niki teased Jomara. "He saw you, too!"

"He coming, Jomara!" Tosha exclaimed.

She saw Talton heading her way, making his way through the crowd. All of sudden she felt shy, looking away like she wasn't paying any attention to the man who was walking towards her. She felt his presence; it was strong and getting stronger by the second. Then she heard him say, "Hey, Block Bleader."

"Huh?" she managed to reply.

Then Niki saved the moment, "What's up, Gangsta? What? You know my homegirl?"

Talton glanced at Niki before directing his gaze back towards his target; "Yeah. We met before."

One thing Jomara couldn't stand was people talking about her while she was standing right there. "How you doin', Talton?"

"Man, I'm good. Blessed. Hey, can I holla at you real quick?"

"Ooohhh..." the girls teased.

"Stop playing," she hissed at her friends. Then to Talton she said, "C'mon," and stepped a few feet out of her team's earshot. "What's good?"

"Everything's straight. You know, getting money, reppin' the set. All that good shit."

Jomara looked him up and down; "All black, huh? Looks like you got something diabolical planned for tonight."

Talton smiled before countering with, "Maybe I like dressing in black."

"Or, maybe you finna put in some work tonight. It really don't matter to me." I respect the game either way."

"As you should. But, yeah, man..."

"Spit it out," Jomara teased him coldly.

"Man, tell a nigga how I can get to know you a little better. You seem hard to find."

"I really ain't that hard to find. I be on the same shit you be on. At least, in my own way."

"That's what's up. As a matter of fact, I meant to ask you 'bout that."

"'Bout what?"

"Where you be getting your work from?"

"Hmmm, maybe I don't wanna expose that information."

Talton snickered. "Okay. I can dig it. But look; remember, you can always stop by the spot and fuck with me. I be on the Ave every day. As a matter of fact, here's my number –"

"Gangsta!" a voice called out from across the parking lot.

$$$$$

M.S. was sitting behind the wheel of his drop 'Stang twiddling with the stereo. He couldn't wait to get the night over with. He had major plans and they needed the right amount of funding. To him, his neighborhood was like a country. A country with its own government, economy and military. Right now, in his eyes, his country wasn't operating at its fullest potential. The Park was big, and for the most part, it was united. It was like one big, extended family. But it could be stronger, according to the way he was viewing things.

Mark was a man on a mission. The most important aspect of his plan was to bring the 'hood together. The first step was to come up on enough to work to make sure everyone was eating. The next move was supplying the whole neighborhood with an arsenal. Individually, most of his homies had fireworks, yet there were still those who didn't have the money to buy heavy metal. He wanted to buy crates for his street marines so they could easily sweep the city of their opps.

He was seriously running all these thoughts through his mind for the umpteenth time when he felt the presence of someone approaching. He instinctively reached for the pistol that was seated on his lap. It didn't matter that he was posted up in a crowd of over 40 Oak Park gang members, M.S. stayed dangerous; self-preservation stayed at the forefront of his mental.

"Blood, you ready?" Insane B asked him when he reached the driver's side. "It's that time." Mark looked at his phone. It was almost 9 p.m. "Yeah. Get everyone together." Mark stepped out the car and looked around. His extra-tall frame gave him a bird's-eye view of the parking lot. Insane was discreetly making his way to all the homies who were gonna ride with them. It seemed as if they were all ready to go. Then he saw Talton off to the side talking to a little Spanish broad with big titties. Mark smiled to himself. His homey was a pussy hound – he stayed in a bitch ear. But it was time to go; "Gangsta!"

Talton turned from the girl to see where his name was being called from. When he saw Mark and they made eye contact, he nodded, said something to the female then started towards his own car.

Insane and Joe Blood came back and got into Mark's car. Moments later, three underworld vehicles slithered through the partygoers and dove into the evening to accomplish their felonious caper...

CHAPTER FOUR
ON-SIGHT ACTIVITIES
"Check out the Crip-blue Chucks!"

–J-Nutty

Ms. Norma was in an uproar! Her middle son, Willie, had gotten in a fight at school and she was in the process of ripping him a new one. The fact that she felt he was in the right for punching on the little boy didn't matter. Being both a mother and a father was a hard job at times.

"Tu vas hacer como tu papa! Sempre estas peleando caundo voi a trabajar par poner comida in la casa! I'm tired of this shit, Willie! Sempre tengo que ir a la escuala a recojerte!"

"But, mami –"

"Shut up!"

"It wasn't my fault!"

"It's always your fault! Ve te de aqui! No te quiero mirrar!"

Something little Willie knew for sure was there was no winning a case when his mother was on a tirade. His only real option in this situation was to wait her out. Frustrated and upset, he went to his room. He was fuming! The kids at school started it all. He couldn't help himself from swinging on the White boy who called him a bastard. Not having a father was one of the sorest

22

subjects in the 8-year old's mental makeup. Just thinking about it made him emotional.

Willie replayed the afternoon's incident in his head a few more times. And just as he started letting the anger of not having a father sink in, his older sister came in the room. From the look on her face he knew he was in for a lecture, but he didn't mind. Jomara always had a way of making him feel good no matter what he was going through. She came in shaking her head, but even that made him feel a little better.

Jomara's heart went out to her little brother. She felt his sadness as soon as she took a seat next to him on the bed. His eyes told it all. He was hurt, yet angry. Angry at the world. "Heard you got in a fight at school. What happened?"

"This kid called me a bastard! They were making fun of me 'cause I ain't got no dad."

"You do got a father," she assured him. "He was a good man, too!"

Willie looked up hoping she would tell him a story about his father. His dad wasn't hers. She was almost 10 years old by the time his mother met his old man. Since he didn't stick around long enough to raise him, little Willie had to grow up hearing stories about him and his escapades. For a quick second he thought she'd start in on another story about him until they were interrupted by their mother screaming, "Jomara! Alguien te hasta llamando!"

"Sis!" said Willie when he saw her about to get up. He didn't want her to leave.

"I'll be right back. Let me go see who it is before mami start fuckin' with my phone. She went to the kitchen where she left her celly on the counter. She didn't recognize the number but she still answered it conscious of the fact that her mother was hovering by trying to eavesdrop. "Hello," she said into the receiver.

"Mara, what you doin'?" asked a familiar voice.

A smile took over her face until she remembered her judgmental mother was nearby. She nonchalantly stepped into the next room and said, "Nothing. My little brother got into it at school so I'm dealing with that."

"Sounds like you need a break."

"I wish."

"You smoke? You wanna ride out?"

Jomara didn't say anything. She wanted to hang out with him. She dug his swagger. He was sexy as fuck. *But, should she?* she asked herself. *Maybe not.*

"Jomara."

"Yeah."

"What's brackin'? You wanna slide out wit' a demon, or what?"

"You don't even know where I live, nigga. I'm not gonna be waitin'–"

"Look outside."

Jomara peeked out the front window and saw Talton sitting behind the wheel of his burgundy Buick. "How did –"

"It's the P. It really ain't that hard to find the new girl."

She smiled. "Okay. Give me a second, tho'." Her mother must have been listening because she quickly came into the living room and said, "You better not stay out too late!" Jomara shook her head. She wasn't surprised one bit. Her overbearing, micromanaging mother was always on her tail. After assuring her that she wouldn't be out long she rushed outside and hopped in the car with Gangsta.

Making sure she didn't pull the curtain too far to the left, Ms. Norma peaked out. She saw the heathen across the street. For no justifiable reason she hated him on sight. Her own relationships with career criminals had her jaded when it came to thugs. Jomara was still young though. She would have to learn on her own. Ms. Norma scoffed before stepping away from the window to go finish dinner.

$$\$\$\$\$\$$$

"Blood! These Air Max's raw!" Terauchi told Kenya. They were at the Foot Locker at the mall in the South area.

"See if they got the same pair in both our sizes," Kenyata replied.

"For real?"

"Relly! I told you I got you!"

Terauchi's smile eclipsed his face before he caught the attention of the Foot Locker clerk. "Hey! You got these in 9 and 10's?"

"I'm pretty sure we do. Let me go check on it for you," the man in the striped shirt replied before stepping away.

Meanwhile, unbeknownst to the duo, there were two teens right outside the Foot Locker studying their presence. They were from Valley High, a neighborhood that had both Crips and Pirus. Cash and J-Nutty were crips whose sole purpose for going to the mall that day was to set trip on anyone not from their 'hood.

"Cuz, check out this Crip-blue chucks!" J-Nutty stated seconds after they entered the shoe store. He made sure to speak extra loud when he continued, "All they need is some fat Crip laces!"

"On Valley High Crip!" Cash interjected just as loud.

Kenya peeped the play immediately. Thoughts of stepping out in brand-new shoes were suddenly forgotten. He looked at his relative and said, "You ready to set-trip?"

"Fo' sho'!" Terauchi replied as he stood up.

Cash and J-Nutty were already on their trail. They all knew what came next. In the middle of the store Cash sized up his opps and said, "What's crackin', cuz?! Y'all got a problem?!"

"Blood, we –" Kenya began before getting cut off by the Foot Locker manager.

"Awww, hell naw! I'm not 'bout to have my shop tore up by some juvenile delinquents!" the middle-aged Black man bellowed from behind the counter. "I'll call security! Fuck all this! Y'all need to get up outta here with this nonsense!"

"On 4th Ave, we can squabble up in the bathroom!" Kenya stated.

"You ain't said shit, cuz!" Cash hissed back.

No more words were necessary. They all understood the assignment. The foursome followed one another to the nearest restroom.

$$$$$

Mark Sanders was the type of man who always had his next move plotted out before the first one was etched in stone. He never had a doubt in his mind the pizza parlor robbery wouldn't happen smoothly. It was simple mathematics; he had an experienced crew of hyenas operating on demon time with him. It was child's play.

He was also at the mall; except he wasn't there to buy some clothes. M.S. and his partna Baca were at the food court enjoying their plates of Panda Express. After doing so much time in prison, a good plate of food was always appreciated. Sometimes it was more enticing than sex.

"Damn, blood!" Baca stated. "This shit good as fuck!"

"I already know," Mark agreed. "Real life sweet-n-sour! God dayum!"

The food court was crowded. Every table was occupied by shoppers chomping on their burgers, tacos, pizza or ice cream. The vibe was cool but that didn't mean it couldn't change course at the drop of a dime. Mark was conscious of this law so he stayed scanning his surroundings. It was a habit of his that saved his life on several occasions.

"So, you think Albertico finna give y'all a good deal?" Baca asked him.

"Damn right! We been fuckin' wit' blood for a minute. It's not even a question in my mind."

"That's what's up!"

Suddenly, Mark's attention was called upon by something he thought he saw across the food court until his vision was blocked by a crowd of people walking by. He waited until his view wasn't obscured before getting a better look and telling Baca, "Ain't that Kenya and 'Rauchi?"

"Where?"

Mark pointed.

"Yeah," Baca said. "Look at Kenya looking like he finna get off in somebody ass. What's wrong wit' blood?"

Mark squinted his eyes, quickly scanning the scene. "Look in front of 'em! They walking with some off-brand niggaz. It looks like they finna get down wit' 'dem niggaz."

"That's exactly what it looks like!"

"C'mon!"

They both got up and quickly crept through the crowds. By the time they got to the restrooms their friends were out of sight. But that didn't mean they were gone. They heard the sound of feet scuffling and bodies slamming against the walls inside the bathroom. Just as they were about to run inside, two older White men rushed out looking disheveled.

They rushed in and found four Pitbulls locked in exchanges of blows. All four teens had hands. They took and gave blammers that would've had the average fighter flinching.

Mark and Baca didn't hesitate. They both dove into the scuffle changing the tide of the altercation. Then something took place that change the melee into a murder scene.

Cash pulled out a pistol and let off a wild shot. The bullet ricocheted off the walls, stopping everyone in their tracks. Everyone except for Mark. Without thinking, he took out his own weapon and started shooting.

BLADADAH! BLADADAH! BLADADAH!

Three green-tipped hollow heads destroyed the young Crip's chest cavity. The world froze for one quick moment. There was no taking back what took place. Mark took something that he couldn't give back before yelling, "C'mon! Let's go!"

The Parksters snapped back to reality and took off running. Everyone within fifty feet of the incident heard the shots. All eyes were on them as they shot through the mall on their way outside. Mall security were on their trail immediately!

It seemed as if they were gonna get away. They were a good distance from the out-of-shape security guards and the exit was coming up with no one in their way. Then all of a sudden Kenya slipped! He slid three feet on the smooth ground before he was able to get back up. But by then it was too late. The security guards were on him.

Terauchi took one last look back as he smashed outside. He wished he could help his cousin, but he couldn't. They ran across the parking lot, got into Mark's Mustang and slithered to safety...

CHAPTER FIVE

FLOWERS FISH MARKET

"I got a question that's been on my mind all day."

−Talton

A few days after the murder at the mall, Talton and Terauchi were at Flowers Fish Market for lunch. They purposely took a spot at a table where they could watch the street without being seen from the outside. It was a habit the streets instilled in certain individuals.

Talton had just washed a mouthful of fried fish down with a gulp of Sprite when he said, "Kenyata been calling all day, every day. Blood is a soldier but it's still fucked up what's happening to him."

"I know," Terauchi replied. His eyes were blood-shot from the sticky he smoked earlier. "It's some fuck-shit fo' sho'. He didn't even do that shit! I mean, there's nothing we can do 'bout it. But, damn."

Gangsta nodded. His silence was filled with meaning. Everyone knew Mark killed Cash, yet Kenya was 'bout to take the fall for it. They all knew Kenyata and how he operated. He came from a cloth that didn't stretch. So there wasn't a doubt in anyone's mind that he'd take a life sentence before removing them Murder Mids stitches off his lips.

"The good news," Talton continued, "is the nigga that got murked was found with a strap next to him when

30

the police came. Kenya's lawyer is pushing for them to check for gun residue on the victim to prove that it was self-defense. That'll turn the murder into a manslaughter."

"Uh-huh," Terauchi replied. Then something outside caught his attention. "Blood, ain't that the Puerto Rican girl you been fuckin' wit' lately?"

Talton looked in the direction of the street just in time to see Jomara step in through the front door. He lit up before he reminded himself to keep his composure. He had hung out with her a few times since he stopped by her house for the first time. Every time he swooped her up, the vibe was straight, but he hadn't really had the chance to fuck with her the way he really wanted to.

She locked eyes with him the moment she stepped into the airconditioned establishment, "Gangsta."

"What's brackin', Mara? What you been –"

"Man, I'm kinda in a hurry. I saw your car outside so I figured I'd step in. You got some work?"

Even though Jomara had stepped close enough not to be heard by evesdroppers, Gangsta still looked around before replying, "Yeah. I got a sack on me. How much you need?"

"All of it."

He looked at her without saying anything. For a split second, he was caught off guard.

But then he smiled and said, "C'mon. Let's go to my car real quick." To his cousin he said, "I'll be right back, blood."

They went outside and got into his car. After shutting the door, Talton reached for a water bottle that was laying on his floor board. The bottle was a stash spot with a secret compartment at the bottom. He unscrewed it, took out his stash and said, "I got thirty-seven –"

"I want it all," she replied. After peeling three hundred and seventy dollars from her bankroll, she handed it to him and said, "I gotta go –"

"Hold up. Hold up, ma! Why you rushing like that?"

"I gotta get this money, Gangsta."

"I feel you, but one thing."

"Yeah."

"When we gonna kick it again?"

Jomara opened the door and was about to get out before she turned to him and asked, "What you doin' tonight?"

"Nothin'. Why?"

"Just asking." She stepped out, shut his door then got in her rental. Talton was sharp but she was too. She pulled into traffic knowing he was watching her drive away. Suddenly, her pussy started dripping. He had that effect on her and she was just about ready to do something about it...

$$$$$

Gangsta was having a good day. He already had to chop up a few extra ounces since money was coming in quick. When he took a break to play some craps on 2nd Ave with the homey Brian, he hit the whole game for thirty-two hundred. Then he got the call from Jomara telling him she had a motel room on Stockton Boulevard. When she gave him the room number and asked him to stop by, Talton was estatic. He already knew what the business was; tonight was the night!

After handling all his business in the streets he went home and got dressed in something crispy. Then before meeting up with her he stopped at Oak Park Market to get a fifth of Yak. When he was paying for his drank, a thought crossed his mind to buy a pack of condoms. He almost did it, but decided against it. In his mind, Jomara was young, sexy and exclusive. She didn't seem ran-through so he felt safe hitting it raw. Of course, he'd pull out before depositing his demon seeds in her. That was a no-brainer; minimum mandatory activities.

Jomara understood the power of pussy, yet chose not to use it. Some of the girls she knew used sex as a bargaining chip. She refused to. She was also well aware of the fact that her punnany was hers and hers only so no one could ever actually say they manipulated her out of a piece of herself. For as long as she could remember, every time she had sex with someone it was because she had made a conscious decision to share herself with a specific man of her choosing.

Talton was one of those cases. She felt a certain attraction to him on their first interaction and hid it. No one would've ever guessed it by her demeanor. Ever since they started hanging out, she got to know him and knew she would take things to the next level when the time came. In her mind, it was a natural progression that her body anticipated aggressively.

She hustled that whole day. The money came fast. She had a nice amount of crack left, yet her stash of cash was worth way more than the product she was holding still. After going to the mall for a new set of sexy lingerie and a bag of bath and body works, she got a motel room on the strip. The most relaxing moment of the evening thus far was when she took a long, warm bubble bath. Then she called Talton. She was still wet when she hit him with her invitation. After smoking a thick blunt to the face she slipped into her new underwear (a black and red ensemble that left her orifices free for a thrashing). Then she waited for a knock on the door to kick off the rest of her evening.

Gangsta was a true player. He didn't even bat an eye when she answered the door half naked. Her curly black hair was long but it couldn't cover her 44 double D's even if she wanted it to. When she turned away from the door and he saw her ass, he smiled. It wasn't Phat Puffs chunky. It was mediocre at best, which he didn't mind. Everything else about her was superb.

When he came out of his clothes, Jomara's eyes bulged at the size of his swipe. She already knew he was packing, but it was different when it was right in her face like that. Jomara's friends had seen the connection early and made it their point to describe what they knew about him. Since Gangsta was born and raised in Oak Park, the size of his piece and the way he used it was public knowledge. Nevertheless, she was glad when he led her to the bed and started feasting on her goods from the back. She already knew she would have to be good and wet before he stuck his swipe in her slit.

Talton dove in immediately after leading her to the edge of the bed and having her get on all fours. He grabbed two handfuls of her ass cheeks, spread them wide and pressed his face into her luscious lower lips.

Jomara had her pussy ate from the back before but this time it was different. Talton was passionate about his assignment. He took his fingers and started stroking her clit after pulling the hood back. It was driving her crazy!

She was loving the feeling he was giving her. Especially when he reached underneath her and fondled her breast. It was good, but at the same time she wanted to feel him in her. "Do it, Talton," she whispered. "Put that dick in me!"

He heard her loud and clear! She was ready for it and he was too! Talton stood up and pressed the head of his aching member halfway into her tight pussy, stretching out her entrance with no remorse.

"Fuuuck!" Jomara moaned upon impact. She was suddenly feeling one of the most pleasurable sensations she had ever experienced in her entire life. Then he pushed another inch of himself inside of her. It felt as if he was splitting her open. But she didn't care. It was exactly what she wanted.

Talton gave her a few seconds and then pushed in a little deeper before withdrawing and then pushing back in. After that he pushed in a little more. With each thrust he was getting deeper inside the sexiest woman he had ever laid eyes one. He took his time eventually getting deep enough to where his hot balls were slapping against her swollen clitoris.

Jomara was on one! Climaxing constantly as he thrusted in and out of her tight snatch. She was now meeting him in mid thrust. "Yeah!" she screamed. "Fuck me, Gangsta! Fuck this pussy, papi!"

"Damn, Mara! I'm 'bout to nut!"

"Cum, papi! Cum! Now!"

Talton wasn't thinkin' when he let loose. He grunted as he shot his load inside her. Jomara started quivering soon after and then he felt her juices dripping onto and down his balls.

When he finally withdrew himself from his Puerto Rican princess, the lovers settled in on top of the covers. She rested her head on his chest as they basked in the ambience of lust.

"You good?" Talton asked her after a while.

"Yeah. Hell yeah. I'm probably gonna be sore in the morning tho'. 'Cause I'm 'bout to get me some more of dat."

Talton laughed.

"I ain't playin'," she said before reaching for his flacid member.

"I see," he commented. A moment of silence passed before he said something else. "Mara."

"What's good, papi?"

"I got a question that's been on my mind all day."

"What's up?"

"I know you got a plug 'cause you was grinding when I met you. That's bool. But for some reason I'm curious why you didn't fuck with him today?"

She took a moment before answering. She was debating on how much information to give him. She liked Talton, but she wasn't naive to the game. Nevertheless, after thinking about it, she felt she could trust him. "Actually... I do got a plug. Albertico is a family friend –"

"Who?" Talton asked quickly.

"Albertico."

"The Cuban? You know Albertico?"

"Yeah," Jomara responded nonchalantly. "We know him from years ago when he lived in Florida."

"Damn! But, why you get a double-up from me when blood got them thangs for the low? He got weight –"

"I don't know. The Ave was jumping and I saw your car in traffic so I decided to stop. Anyways, he don't show that much love. He would've had me waiting all day." She hoped he couldn't see through her deception. The fact of the matter was Albertico did give her better deals. She had ran out of work and could've easily stopped by his house for more. The reason she chose not to was because she had wanted to see Talton. She really liked him so she didn't mind putting money in his pocket. "Why you asking? You think I'm the laws or something?"

"Naw," Talton chuckled. "Naw, baby... You far from the law. You one of the realest females I met in a while..."

CHAPTER SIX

SIDE STREETS

"I know this nigga don't think he gonna get some pussy then bounce!"

–Jomara

"On Cash Loc, C.I.P., I'ma catch one of them Orange Peel-ass niggaz!" Big Snake told his younger homies when they first embarked on their murderous mission to catch an opp slippin'.

From the passenger seat, J-Nutty pulled his .45 from his waistband and placed it on his lap. "Fuck 'dem niggas, cuz! I'ma ride every night till I smack at least two of them niggaz!"

The streets took over whenever the sun gave in. It almost seemed as if Sacramento's street lights offered all the illumination needed for the underworld to operate off of.

Like an extra ripe onion, the underworld has many layers. The dope game bread D-Boys. Jackers operated in an industry with no guidelines, committing home invasions and robberies. There were pimps, hoes, drug addicts and sliders who passed with white collar crimes. They all loved and specialized in their careers. The one thing they all shared was the fact they all embraced the stitch-lipped customs of this sub-culture called the Game.

Gangland was another aspect of the mean streets of California's capital. Just like any other way of life or profession, there are many different levels of participation based on experience and individual temperament.

On the lighter, more visible level there were gang members. There's a difference between gang members and gang bangers. The thugs who dressed the part and went to all the city's night clubs and other functions are the "members." They're the one's who're most likely to be seen in a YouTube video set-trippin'.

Then there's the real bangers. Bangers are the real active members who live for putting in work. They slide when it's time to ride. No one has to tell them or pressure them to do anything because they love the Game.

Big Snake was a gang banger. He was a reputable Valley High Crip whose resume included four confirmed kills. Cash was his baby mamma's younger brother. His two little homies, J-Nutty and Smokes were Cash's everyday niggaz, so it made sense for them to unite for the night-time hunt.

They had been riding around the city for close to an hour by the time they decided to stop at a gas station on Franklin Boulevard for some dranks and a Swisher. Other, less motivated demons would've called it a night after creeping for that long without a sighting. That wouldn't be the case for that carload of bangers. Big Snake was dead serious about his gangland movements. He lived for the sound of his gun coughing. The searching, shooting and confirmation of death was a high that he chased with the passion of a meth addict fiending for a fix.

They were parked on the dark side of the gas station they stopped at when Smokes took a snort from his coke sack and passed it to J-Nutty. "Cuz, I'm lit! On Cash, I'ma make one of them nigga's mamma's cry like my nigga's mamma cried!"

J-Nutty shook his head after taking a hit from the sack. His memory was plagued with scenes of his homey dying along with his mother crying as if her own life had ended. Without realizing what he was doing, he squeezed his burner extra tight. He wouldn't rest till he got a kill. He promised himself that the moment he saw his best friend's soul escape his arms, legs and head.

Snake stayed scanning the shadows. He was more analytical about this drill than the younger, less experienced Locs he was riding with. They were emotionally involved, which was cool. Their emotions would fuel their trigger fingers. His motivation came from a different set of factors. As far as he was concerned it was business. Gangland politics. Someone from Oak Park took the life of a Valley High Crip. Technically, the laws of the land dictated retaliation, and anyone from the P was fair game. It was written in the street code.

"That's right, Crip!" Snake replied to Smokes' comment. "We gonna make a nigga's mamma cry. But check this out, cuz. There's different types of kills we can make right now."

"What'chu mean?" J-Nutty asked.

"A'ight. Check it: We can ride through Smoke Park, catch a random slob and knock his noodles out, right?"

"On Crip!" Smokes agreed.

"It'll be a kill. One slob down," Snake explained. "But there's another way to look at it. See, if we murk a random nigga, there really won't be a confirmation in the streets that we did it. The P is a big set with all kinds of enemies. Anybody can ride up and catch a body if they drummin' like that. They so deep, there's a chance we can catch a nobody-ass nigga that no one gives a fuck about, and then it won't mean shit. But think about the mark we'll make if we bury one of the niggaz who was actually there that day."

"That'll hurt 'em," J-Nutty commented.

"From the description you gave us," Snake told Nutty, "It was Oak Park Mark who pulled the trigger. Cuz is a factor in his 'hood. We'll get a Crip-Blue trophy for knocking that nigga out the box with this drumroll!"

"On Cash!" the younger Crips agreed.

"See what I'm sayin'?" With that, he started his car and pulled into traffic. The evening was still young with all kinds of possibilities. Then, not long after continuing the hunt, J-Nutty saw something and demanded Snake's attention.

"Cuz! Look at that car! Look, cuz! That nigga in the passenger seat was the slob I squabbled up wit' at the mall!

Snake saw the car his partna was pointing at. It passed them up, going in the opposite direction. "You sure?"

"On Cash! It's him, cuz!"

The older Crip slammed his foot on the brake and made an illegal U-turn. He knew better than to commit a petty traffic infraction while riding dirty, but this was one of those opportunities that didn't display itself on a daily basis.

$$$$$

Jomara studied her naked torso in the mirror. Her extra-large titties were perky as they could be despite their size. Her flat stomach was sexy as well. She was bad and she knew it. Before she went back into the room, she took one last look at herself and smiled. She couldn't wait to get back to her thug.

Talton was at the edge of the bed putting his pants back on. *Hell naw!* she thought to herself when she realized what he was doing. "What's goin' on?" she asked, trying to mask her sudden rage. *I know this nigga don't think he's gonna get some pussy then bounce!*

"Put your clothes on. The relly just called. His car broke down so I'm finna go get 'im."

"Oh," she said. "Okay. Hold on."

"I hope you not one of them females that be taking an hour to get ready," Talton teased.

"That's not me, Gangsta."

She slid her jeans and shirt on in record time. Her curly hair went into a loose bun and they were ready to go.

It didn't take them long to pull up on his younger cousin Terauchi. She already knew him so it didn't bother her when Talton asked her to get in the back seat so he could talk to his relative.

Jomara was feeling Talton. She watched him from the back seat and shook her head when she secretly thought, *Ughh. This nigga sexy as fuck and he knows it!*

"... Yeah, nigga, renting dope fiend's cars is dangerous if you don't know how it runs. That muthafucka had you stranded near the 'hood this time. But what if you would've been out of bounds?"

"I know, blood. That's why I need my own shit. I'm ready to get me something clean."

"Shiiit. Once this deal goes down, I'll put enough work in your hand to put you in a position to buy your own car."

"So, Albertico finna match y'all?" Terauchi asked. As soon as the words left his mouth, he knew it was a mistake. Talton cut his eyes at him, sending a silent message to dead the conversation.

Jomara was cool, but he didn't know her good enough to give her classified information. "We got shit lined up, relly. What's so bool 'bout it is how we all working together. This Park shit runs deep."

"On Bloods!"

Talton glanced at Jomara from the rear-view mirror. He actually caught her staring at him and smiled at how fast she looked away. He liked her ism. She had obviously been raised by thugs by the way she operated on demon time. Then, just as he was about to look away, something else caught his attention. In the distance, a dark four-door had made a reckless move in traffic. He didn't recognize the vehicle and it wasn't close enough to be a threat, but still. He made a mental note to keep an eye on it.

"So, who was you creepin' wit'?" Talton asked Terauchi.

"No one."

Jomara laughed loud enough for both of them to hear.

"What's so funny?" Terauchi asked.

"You! Nigga!" she teased. "I already know who lives in them apartments you was standing in front of."

"Who?" Talton asked.

"Ebony," she challenged Terauchi. "Tell me I'm lying, nigga!"

A sly smile crept across his face.

"Damn, nigga!" Talton exclaimed. "You fuckin' on Ebony's thick ass?"

"Naw. It ain't even like that," Terauchi lied.

"Mmm-hmmm," Jomara kidded from the back seat.

"Okay," Terauchi countered. "What about you? You fuckin' my relly, or what?"

Jomara shut her facial expressions down real quick. Not quick enough to hide her blush, yet fast enough to stay stitched-lipped 'bout the situation.

"I knew it!" Terauchi teased.

Talton looked at Jomara through the rear-view again. They exchanged a silent understanding.

No words were needed in a situation only lovers would understand. It was a vibe but it didn't last long. Something had caught Talton's attention.

The same dark sedan he saw earlier was on his tail. It wasn't close enough to be a for-sure threat, but something about it seemed sketchy.

"Check it," Talton announced in a serious tone. "There's a car behind us that looks shady. I'ma bend a few side streets to see if they still follow us. If it's nothing, it's nothing. But if they following us, this shit can get ugly."

Terauchi took his pistol out of the large packet in the front of his hooded Chicago Bulls Sweatshirt. Jomara wished she could do the same, but couldn't because she left her heater at home that day. Regardless, she felt safe. Talton and his cousin were goonies; they could defend themselves along with anyone else they loved. What bothered her about the situation was the fact that she couldn't activate since she didn't have her gun on her.

"Jomara," Talton said.

"Yeah."

"These muthafuckaz is on us. I'm not sure who it is, but they not homies tho'."

She nodded.

"When I hit the next corner I'ma need you to hop out the car. Stay low. Get behind a tree, a car, or in somebody yard. It's gonna be some shit, 'Mara. So be ready."

"A'ight," she said before scooting next to her escape hatch.

Terauchi cocked his pistol, chambering a round. Gangsta reached underneath his seat, grabbed his metal and did the same.

Jomara looked out the back window. The car in question was right behind them. Talton had took too many side streets for them not to be following them with ill intentions. Her adrenaline started pumping. She knew it was about to get spicy.

"You ready?" Talton asked.

"Yeah!" she replied.

Suddenly, the car sped up the hit a hard right turn. "Now! Jomara, now!" Terauchi demanded.

She opened the door and threw herself onto the asphalt. After a rough tumble, she got on her feet and ran behind a parked car.

That's when the fireworks started. The dark four-door hit the corner with two men hanging out its

45

windows on opposite sides with guns pointed towards Talton's Buick.

BLOCKA! BLOCKA! BLOCKA!

BLADADAH! BLADADAH! BLADADAH!

Both cars exchanged gunfire with one another. The night's calm had been shattered by gunshots and screeching tires.

She took off running the moment they were out of view. She knew where she was. Her house was only a few blocks away. Talton must've considered that when he came up with the idea for her to get out the car. Still, she ran. She ran and ran until she made it home...

CHAPTER SEVEN

BURNT BRIDGES

"In the trenches, twists and turns often bring sad surprises...."

– King Guru

It takes a certain caliber of street nigga to wake up early on a daily basis. It's usually the ones who are serious 'bout their bag chase. Gangsta was one of the types who was cultivated from that type of soil. On top of that, his addiction to the Game fueled his daily rise.

The highspeed shootout didn't last long. Shots were fired back and forth while they raced through the Mids. Then suddenly the dark sedan pulled back. Talton didn't take the time to mull over the reason for his antagonizers to retreat. Instead, he dropped Terauchi off and rushed back to the room Jomara had gotten.

If there was something he knew very well about his neighborhood, it was that the patrol officers were aggressive. Hanging out after a shootout was a definite no-no in the P. Loitering after felonies would have you waking up in the county jail.

The first thing he did when he got up was reach for his phone. Talton wiped the sleep from his eyes, getting ready for the light from the screen to assault his unfocused eyes. But it didn't happen because his phone never came on. The battery was dead.

"Fuck," he muttered to himself as he sat up in bed. The charger was in the car. *Fuck it. I gotta get up anyway,* he thought. Talton had woken up to a warehouse full of shooting thoughts. Anyone else would've shown signs of stress. Not him. Turmoil was natural for a man who thrived in muck mixed with sex, money and murder.

After washing his face and taking his morning shit, Talton got ready to leave. He smiled to himself when he sat on the edge of the bed to put his shoes on. He really liked Jomara. He needed to check up on her to make sure she got home safely. She was really starting to grow on him and that didn't happen too often.

She was a soldier. He was impressed by the way she moved. When she didn't panic when things got spicy the night before, it just cemented his assumptions that she had experience in the trenches. The Puerto Rican temptress was obviously brought up in soil just as dirty as the Park's and he loved it.

He didn't let his thoughts linger for too long. He had business to handle. No time to mentally cupcake with fresh memories. Gangsta stepped out and headed to his car. *Damn*, he thought when he saw her rental parked next to his scraper. Another reminder to check up on the girl who roughly tumbled out of his car the night before.

"Talton!" a woman's voice called out from behind him as he was about to get into his whip. "Gangsta, is that you?!?"

When he turned around, he was met with a face from his past. A female he never thought he'd see again.

Angel...

"Oh my God!" exclaimed Talton's teenage crush. Without warning she rushed towards him and planted a long, intimate kiss on his mouth.

Gangsta was caught completely off guard. His shock of suddenly seeing her had him off his square for a second. When he got ahold of himself, he pushed her away and wiped his mouth in disgust.

She had missed the signs of his discomfort because she asked, "When did you get out?" like they were old friends.

"Huh?" he said. "When did you get back?"

"I been around for a minute. I had a baby." Suddenly, her voice got a little lower as she subconsciously looked away for a fraction of a second. "She stays with my mamma."

A stampede of memories bulldozed through Gangsta's frontal lobe. He was once madly in love with this woman. She was the baddest bitch of his generation in their teens. They fell in love on some Bonnie and Clyde shit. It all ended when a judge broke them up. He got locked up and she couldn't handle a long-distance relationship. He had forced himself to forget her because of the effect of her abandoning him had on his on his mental.

Suddenly, his subconscious sent a feeling akin to his chest caving in. He was taken back to all the afternoons in CYA with no mail and all the refused collect calls he made. Then, just as fast as they came, they left, and he was back to the here and now.

Talton scanned her person with his eyes. High heels. Short skirt. Dirty nails. Cheap weave. Way too much lip gloss.

Ho-bitch.

"... So, yeah, me and Manny been travelling a lot lately."

"Manny?" Talton asked. "Why is that name so familiar?"

"Everybody calls him Manny Fresh. He's on his way to come pick me up right now. As a matter of fact, there he go."

A black Impala on 24s pulled into the parking lot and stopped several yards away from them. As soon as he saw the car he realized who her man was. Manny was a pimp from the Bay Area. A young Richmond nigga about his bread.

Gangsta watched Angel scurry to the Impala's passenger side and get in after waving at him. He nodded before getting into his own car. Talton shook his head at the thought of how things turned out. The Game was funny sometimes. In the trenches, twists and turns often bring about sad surprises...

$$$$$

"Girl, you keep rubbin' that thigh like you in major pain," Niki kidded Jomara.

"This shit hurt, bitch. I swear to God I had to dive out of a moving vehicle," Jomara replied from Niki's passenger seat. Then she looked at her phone for what seemed like the hundredth time that morning, hoping she'd get a call from her man.

"I don't know what else to do, 'Mara. We went by his spot, all his niggas' spots and his Granny's house."

"I know. The bitch at the booking desk said he wasn't in jail, either. I don't know, man. I just hope he's okay."

Jomara stared out the window. It felt like they had circled the Murder Mids six times in their search for Gangsta. She had blown up his phone from the moment she woke up that morning. It would've been one thing if the phone would have at least rang, she told herself. But the fact that it was going straight to voicemail is what had her so vexed.

Niki glanced at her friend. Jomara looked distraught. In the short time she'd known the Puerto Rican transplant, she had learned to admire her for her strength and her I-don't-give-a-fuck attitude. She was a stone with sharp edges. Her emotions rarely came to surface.

"So, tell me again, bitch. That nigga blow them guts out, or what?" Niki asked, trying to lighten the mood a little. "What hurts more? Your coochie or your thigh?"

Jomara laughed. She couldn't help herself. "Bitch! I didn't tell you shit like that."

"I know. But you can tell me now. Where he take you? He probably took you to the Marriott –" Suddenly, Niki stopped in her tracks. She slammed her foot on the brake in front of a house on 6th Ave right next to a small alley that led to the Big Park. Something about Jomara's face made her think something and she needed immediate clarification. "I know you didn't let the nigga fuck you in his car!"

"What da fuck!?! You trippin'! We had a room!" Then, just as the words left her mouth, she remembered her car. "Fuck!"

"What, bitch?"

"I left my rental at the room!"

51

"What room?"

"Go to Stockton! I had got a room on Stockton Boulevard!"

"You think he went back to it?" Niki asked while putting the car back in gear.

"I don't know. Maybe. I wasn't even thinking 'bout that shit. I forgot all about the car and the room. Shit, the car might not even be there 'cause I left the keys in the sun visor with the door unlocked."

Niki smiled to herself. Jomara was something else. Real ghetto. But that was the main reason they clicked.

Stockton Boulevard wasn't far at all. They made it to the motel in record time. "That's it right there, right?" Niki asked as she slowed down and got ready to pull into the parking lot. "Hold up! Ain't that Gangsta right there?"

Jomara looked and saw him. There was a female approaching him. "Hold on. Don't go in yet." She didn't know why she said it, but she did. A second later, they both saw something that broke and shattered Jomara's seasoned heart. Gangsta was giving some random bitch a deep, passionate kiss. The fact that they hadn't kissed with such passion the night before told Jomara exactly where she stood in his life.

"Go!"

"What?" Niki asked.

"Go! Fuck that nigga!" Jomara growled. She fought with all her might to not cry. Her voice had cracked towards the end of that sentence.

Niki watched her friend's heart shatter right beside her. She knew the devastation Jomara was experiencing because she had her heart strings snatched out before too.

If she would've chosen to beat the other bitch's ass, Niki would have rocked with her. That was her homegirl, right or wrong. Good and bad. But if leaving was what she wanted, then bouncing is what they would do.

Jomara stared off into the distance not really seeing anything. She should have known Talton was a dog! It was too good to be true. Jomara's head started spinning from the anger she was experiencing. She felt robbed. She felt betrayed.

"Mara."

"Yeah."

"Where you wanna go?"

"I don't know. Can you just drive..."

CHAPTER EIGHT

BLACK BEANS & RICE

"I'ma go ahead and get some baking soda so we don't gotta stop on the way back."

– Oak Park Mark

Life in the trenches moved fast. Talton went straight to his house on 4th Ave, took a shower and made some calls before heading out with M.S. It was a big day since the duo were about to cop a kilo of coke for their team. Then, after bringing the work back to the trap, they planned on spending the rest of the afternoon cooking it into double the amount in crack.

When M.S. pulled up to Talton's house, Gangsta was already outside waiting for him with a black leather bag, holding their investment money. Talton got in and Mark took off. After taking his nine out and tucking it under the seat, Talton leaned back and took a deep breath. There was a lot on his mind, yet no way to let it out.

Mark watched his old friend. Talton was a real nigga, one who could be counted on. Mark loved him for that. They had been through a lot together since their early years so he could tell when something was up with him. The car had barely started moving by the time Mark detected the strain on his goon's mental. Talton wasn't one to display his emotions, but when he did, it was because of something serious. It was obvious this was one of those times so he decided to address it. "Nigga, what's up wit' you? Don't tell me them suckaz got you shook up?"

"Fuck naw! We already know things go pop in the night. That shit wasn't shit. But, for real, whoever it was was bold. Feeling comfortable enough to come that deep up in the 'hood is slick shit."

"Yeah..." Mark replied. He cut his eyes towards Gangsta trying to study his facial expressions.

There had to be more on his friend's mind. "It's obvious we at war. But wit' who? You still don't know?"

Talton shook his head while he stared off into the distance. "I didn't get a good look. I swear I was looking hard, too. I can recognize the car if I saw it again, but I didn't get a good look at who it was."

"It had to be some of them Valley High niggaz. They gotta be hot 'bout what happened to they homey. I been seeing T-shirts wit' that nigga's face 'round town lately. You know the only time you see muthafucka's faces on apparel is when they was somebody to his people."

It was Talton's turn to turn and study Mark's profile. Kenya was sitting in jail for something he didn't do. The whole conversation was reminding him of that. For some reason, he experienced a sense of hostility towards the man he was sitting in the car next to. He let it go though.

Situations like these happened all the time. It was part of the life. He couldn't blame Mark for Kenyata's slip and fall. No one could.

Mark kept studying his friend. Something was up but he couldn't quite place it and it was beginning to vex him. In his eyes, a person's survival depended on how much he knew about his surroundings and the people in it. He had seen some of the most dangerous individuals he knew taken down by individuals in his inner circle. Both directly and indirectly.

"Why you keep lookin' at your phone?" Mark asked.

"I'm tryna catch up wit' Jomara –"

"Who? The Puerto Rican girl you been hanging out wit'?"

"She was wit' us last night. Still ain't heard from her. I've been trying to hit her up but she ain't answering."

"I know you don't think she set y'all up, right?"

"Naw! Fuck no! It's just weird she's not picking up her phone."

So that's it, huh, thought Mark. *The lil' bitch got the homey fucked up.* "You need to get your head in the game, blood. We got business to handle."

"Yeah. I know. I'm good." Talton sat up a little straighter. Mark was right. Jomara was thugged out. She could take of herself; he didn't have to worry bout her. *Little baby probably lost her phone when she hopped out the car last night*, he thought to himself. He made a mental note to stop by her house after he handled everything in the streets, then he pushed her file to the back of his mind.

Mark pulled up to a small corner store in the P. "Hold up real quick. I'ma go ahead and get us some baking soda so we don't gotta stop on the way back."

"Bet."

$$\$\$\$\$\$$

Snake was at his best when he slithered through Sac with his strap on his lap. His addiction to clappin' was akin to that of an adrenaline junky. There wasn't much of a difference between him and someone who parachuted out of a low flying plane on a stormy night. He lived for the rush; he loved the sound of his gun bustin'.

He had barely slept since the chase he was forced to abort the evening before. One of the bullets ricocheted off the asphalt, blowing out his front tire. If his opps would've realized what happened he was sure he would've taken a loss. They probably wouldn't have made it out the ghetto alive.

Luckily one of his little homies had an auntie who lived in the Mids. They barely made it there and were able to tuck the car underneath a tarp. It was a blessing that Snake was wise enough to recognize. But it did nothing to alleviate the nagging feeling that he had fucked up. His targets had gotten away. That alone drove him into a rage. Snake was a Grim Reaper-type nigga. He always got his man.

Always!

Thus, he was still on the hunt. Except this time, he decided to enlist the assistance of one of his more experienced niggaz. His little homies were more than willing to slide. They wanted to go home and rest though. Snake wasn't trying to wait. The murder was on his mind like the nagging of someone with OCD. Instead of sleeping or showering, he stayed on the move.

Snake was in the passenger seat of his partna Twist's Chevy Van. Twist was one of his niggaz from the sandbox. He had a nice van with tinted windows they could spy from behind.

It was a clean ride with rims, beat and a hideaway bed in the back. It wasn't a ride they would shoot from but it served its purpose on reconnaissance missions in the battle field.

Since Oak Park was where his opps were from, Oak Park was where they hunted. The P was a big neighborhood with a lot of back alleys and side streets. Finding a random gang member lackin' wouldn't be that hard. But locating random targets wasn't what he was on.

The evening before brought him in contact with Gangsta from 4th Avenue. He knew exactly who he was from doing time with him at the Boys Ranch years earlier. The homies had described Mark Sanders as the shooter. And now, it was all beginning to make sense. They were dealing with a specific set of Parksters. It was a clique from Pebble Beach.

As a full-time gang banger, it was Big Snake's job to know all the reputables from every 'hood in his city. Mark and Gangsta were the type of individuals who made a difference in the streets. When they were home, which wasn't often since they stayed incarcerated, the streets were guaranteed to stay lit.

Sacramento's street life was an established subculture operating just under the surface of where law abiding citizens lived. Everyone who was anyone knew one another. That's why and how Snake and Twist knew exactly who they were searching for. They could've driven past 50 different Oak Park Bloods and not reacted because they knew exactly who they were trying to catch. And neither one of them rushed the process since they knew the niggaz they were looking for stayed in the mix. They were the types who were always outside. The streets were their playground.

That's why when they spotted Mark's Mustang in traffic, neither one of them saw the situation as a stroke of luck. On the contrary, it was all mathematical. Reputables weren't hard to find.

"Got 'im!" Twist announced when he spotted the 'Stang. "Ain't that Oak Park Mark's whip right there?"

Snake took a good look across the intersection. "Damn right! And he got Gangsta wit' 'im! On Crip, we got 'em!"

"Don't even trip, cuz! As soon as they pull up on a side street, we'll activate on they ass!"

"Slob-ass niggaz!" Snake made sure his Glock was chambered and ready to shoot. This time, he was determined to hit his mark. "I'ma walk right up on them slobs!"

"On Cash Loc!"

Twist followed them from a safe distance. The Mustang was heading towards Downtown. Ideally, a residential setting was the best spot to kill someone. But just because they were heading Downtown didn't mean they were heading towards the business district. There were all kinds of houses and apartments out there.

They followed Gangsta and Mark for a cool minute before they arrived where they were going. It was the perfect setting for a murder. A quiet area with no one outside to witness the gangland ambush. Twist parked up the street from where Mark pulled up at. They sat in the van and watched them for a moment before Snake said, "Cuz, you see that nigga –"

"Backpack?"

"Yeah. You know both them niggaz be getting money. It could be anything in that bag."

Snake thought for a moment. They were there to up the scorecard. Money had nothing to do with it. Yet, as soon as money entered the equation, everything was a lot more enticing.

After sliding their ski masks on, the Crips got out the van and made their way towards the Mustang. They found a safe spot behind some bushes in front of the apartment building Mark and Talton had entered, then waited. It was a bold move since it was broad daylight. They weren't nervous though. Both of them understood the assignment and were more than willing to accept the risk.

$$$$$

When Gangsta and Mark entered Albertico's spot, the vibe was smooth. It was all smiles; business mixed with pleasure. After a few drinks along with a plate of black beans and rice, they stepped out their plug's apartment with just over two kilos of cocaine in Gangsta's leather backpack. Things couldn't have went better. Albertico had been more than willing to front them the same amount they paid for. He didn't even raise the price based on the issue of consignment. A real player deal.

They walked out with the bag in Mark's hand. The moment they knew they weren't within the Cuban's earshot they gave each other dap and quietly celebrated.

"It's time to eat, nigga!" Mark said.

"On Bloods, whoop! It's on –"

"Say, cuz!" a voice announced from behind them.

Then, before either of them could process the hostility behind the voice, the deafening roar of a Glock 17 started hitting its drumline.

BLOCKA! BLOCKA! BLOCKA!

On instinct, Talton pulled out his blaster and started clapping back!

YACKA! YACKA! YACKA! YACKA!

Mark reached for his own metal but caught a hot one to the shoulder that knocked him down. He scrambled to catch his footing while gunshots rang out from all around him. His shoulder was burning. He looked for cover and dove towards the nearest vehicle. The whole time he was conscious of his wound, hoping an artery wasn't severed.

The shots were coming from two different shooters. Talton had to find cover as well. Half of him was more concerned for his fallen comrade than his own well-being. As soon as he got next to Mark he asked him, "Blood, you alright?"

BLOCKA! BLOCKA! BLOCKA! BLOCKA!

Bullets whizzed by both of their heads. The sound of hollow tips penetrating the car they were squatting behind echoed in their ears.

Mark handed Talton his strap and said, "Get 'em up off us, blood!"

Gangsta hopped up with two heaters in his paws. He relentlessly started letting off in the direction of his attackers. Shots rang out, keeping the once-quiet block lit like a war zone.

Then, just like the night before, his opps retreated. He watched as they ran away from his incoming gunfire. They hopped into a van and started backing up the block in reverse. He kept shooting, chasing them as far as he could before they hit the corner and burnt rubber on their way to wherever they came from.

Albertico came running into the mix with two of his relatives behind him carrying heavy metal. Talton saw them wishing they had showed up thirty seconds earlier. Then something made him look towards the spot where the ambush took place. There was something about the way they ran away from him that had him thinking. He couldn't really tell, but it almost seemed as if one of them was carrying something. After scanning the walkway where they got caught slipping, Talton rushed to Mark's side and asked him, "Blood, where's the work?"

Mark looked at him with anger in his eyes. There's no way them niggaz got their shit! "Help me up, whoop!"

CHAPTER NINE

SILENT TEARS

"You gotta watch these bitches, bruh."
– Ant

Albertico rushed towards Gangsta and Mark. As soon as he saw the hole in Marks shirt, he barked some orders in Spanish that caused goons to round the duo up and lead them to an all-white SUV. They didn't know where they were being taken. It wasn't a hospital, yet they were assured Mark would be taken care of. Less than fifteen minutes later, they parked in front of another home not far from Albertico's. They were then led into an apartment that belonged to an older Spanish man with a lot of hospital equipment. It was obvious the older man had experience taking care of wounded soldiers by the way he swiftly took control of the situation the moment they arrived.

Their plug's relatives didn't stick around. They left Talton and Mark in the care of the doctor without any sort of introductions whatsoever. Mark was livid! He was chattering nonstop. Which was a good thing since it meant the wounds weren't lethal.

It didn't take long for the diagnosis to come in. According to the underworld surgeon the bullet hit a bone in Mark's shoulder and bounced right back out. The end result was two clean holes in Mark's upper chest. It looked as if M.S. would be good after he got cleaned up and patched up.

Talton was hot too. They got caught lackin' in the worst way possible. His head was starting to hurt from thinking too much. He needed some sort of peace in order to get his thoughts together. He stepped outside onto the porch to get some air and clear his mind.

Once he was outside, a face appeared in his thoughts. Jomara! She always had a cool vibe. Plus he hadn't heard from her since the night before. He took a seat on railing overlooking the sidewalk and called her phone. That call was answered on the third ring.

"What!?"

"Damn!" Talton remarked after hearing the way she answered the phone. "You good? Where you been?"

"I been at home," she shot back hotly.

Ignoring the attitude, Talton continued, "Man, the last 24 hours been brazy! Last night was fucked up –"

"What do you want, Talton?" Jomara cut in, regretting opening her legs to this man.

Again, he ignored the attitude, assuming he was somehow interpreting her words incorrectly. "Me and Mark just got robbed!"

"What?!"

"Yeah! we just got in a big-ass shootout in front of Albertico's spot. We went over there to handle some business, and when we came out –"

"You got robbed! Ha!"

Now, that was obvious disrespect, thought Talton. Time to reevaluate some things 'cause Jomara was on some other shit.

"How does it feel to get played, nigga? What goes around comes around, huh?"

"What?!" Talton asked, clearly dumbfound.

"Bitch-ass nigga! Think I'm just gonna sit back and let you play me without clappin' back? You got me fucked up! Fuck you!"

Jomara hung up the phone right before her voice cracked. There was no way in hell she would give him the satisfaction of hearing her anguish spill.

She was devastated. She kept seeing him hugged up and kissing that bitch at the motel. She couldn't believe herself for falling for him. *Fuck dat bitch-ass nigga,* she thought to herself. Still, she knew she was wrong for implying she had something to do with what happened to him. She knew the game well enough to realize she had put herself in the middle of a mix she knew nothing about. She didn't care though. She was angry and didn't give a fuck about what Talton was going through.

A few moments passed before she let her emotions take over. She buried her face in her hands and cried. She let out deep, loud sobs. She was so caught up in her anguish that she didn't see her mother ushering her younger brother from the doorway to her bedroom.

Ms. Norma couldn't do anything but shake her head in disappointment. Single motherhood had left its impression on the older woman. In her world, heartbreak was inevitable. Even necessary at times. In a world as cold as the one she lived in, one needed to cultivate a certain hardness in order to navigate through murky waters.

Gangsta sat there staring at his phone for a minute. He couldn't believe what she said and how she hung up on him. After a while, a discarded tire in the vacant lot across the street from where he was seated demanded all his attention. His jaws were clenched. He was beyond vexed at the hostility he was just met with. *What the fuck is she talking 'bout? We was cool last night*, he thought to himself. Then, even more questions began to materialize. Could he really have been set up. Had she been fake with him the whole time?

Then he remembered talking to Terauchi about their deal with Albertico. Jomara had been right there listening to the whole exchange. *Damn!* he thought. She was given enough intel to set him up if she wanted to. Was it possible that he got played like a rookie?

That's about the time his phone vibrated. He was so mad he didn't even look at the screen before answering. "Yeah."

"Gangsta!" Ant, Talton's older brother said from the other end of the country.

"Blood," Talton replied sounding downtrodden.

"What da fuck wrong wit' you, brody? You sounding like the Feds just indicted the whole 'hood!"

"Naw, bro. It's just hella shit been transpiring these last few days. Last night, some suckaz clapped at me and 'Rauchi in traffic. Then, just now, me and Mark got robbed for two bricks! Shit ugly right now."

Ant didn't reply just yet. He took in everything Talton was telling him, at the same time giving him an opportunity to vent. Something he knew was worth a lot in a world where not many people gave a fuck about the next man.

"... Then, this bitch I been fuckin' wit' just said some shit like she the one who set a nigga up –"

"Wait. What?"

"Man, I don't know what's going on. I was just wit' the bitch last night when we got in the shootout. We split up and I hadn't heard from her till just now. Then, out of nowhere she started flashing. Talkin' 'bout what goes around comes around type shit."

"You gotta watch these bitches, bruh. Look how Alicia did me. When I brought her to Florida she didn't know nobody. Barely even knew how to talk English. But then, after she got settled in and made some friends she started fagging off."

"I didn't know she was on some dumb shit. She had your back when y'all was living out here."

"Yeah. But shit changes, bruh. Bitches switch up like the weather. Talton, don't ever trust a bitch. They just like niggaz, 'cept they got a pussy!"

"I know, blood. I know."

"Another thing. It sounds like shit getting hot out there. You know you can come to Florida anytime you want, right? I'm just living a square life with a 9 to 5. But at least a nigga don't gotta look over his shoulder every sixteen seconds.

"I feel you, brody. On Park Gang, I'ma keep that in mind. But, right now it's spicy in the trenches. It looks like we gotta press play on some suckaz. I can't see myself bouncing during funk season. Feel me?"

"On Bloods."

"A'ight, brody. I gotta go."

"Take care, lil bro. I love you!"

"Love you too!"

CHAPTER TEN

PILLOW TALK

"We got a line on the niggaz that robbed us."
– Oak Park Mark

Over a week and a half had passed since Mark had been shot. The whole Park knew there was a war in the midst. Word circulated with assumptions as to who their immediate opposing faction was, yet no one had concrete proof as to who it was who was taking pot shots at them. Everyone assumed it was Valley High, though. Since Cash had been killed by one of their own, it was the obvious choice. Still, no one actually knew for sure.

That was until some pillow talk crawled out the bedroom...

$$$$$

Insane B was one of the niggaz who stayed on the front lines. He was one of Mark's most loyal disciples, putting him at the helm of every mix. Even when he wasn't in the trenches, he was still in war mode. An active gang banger.

B was laid up with a female from Fruitridge on the second floor of the Marriott basking in the ambience of a recent cock thrashing. The sheets were doused from pussy making the room smell of sex mixed with Runtz.

The stress of the streets wasn't on either one of their minds as Insane channel surfed the room's cable channels.

"Oh my god, boo," Lynette started. "You got this pussy throbbing!"

B smiled. He went brazy in the coochie. Knowing what he did, an affirmation wasn't needed. Nevertheless, the accolades were welcomed.

"You know what?" she continued. "I wanna get you something."

"Huh?" he mumbled. *Now, this what I'm talking 'bout*, he secretly thought to himself.

"For real! I was looking at the new J's and I wanna get us a matching pair."

"Say more."

"Shit, my cousin been braggin' 'bout how much money he got right now. So, I know it won't be shit for him to shoot me a few notes."

"What cousin?" B asked, not really giving a fuck.

"My relly, Twist. That nigga's always coming up on something."

Now, this got B's attention. The name Twist rang a bell but he couldn't quite place it. "He bang?"

"He from Valley High. Anyways, he came up on a lick a couple weeks back –"

Insane sat up, giving his jump-off all his attention. The mention of a jux forced him to take notes. He wasn't really sure where the current topic was going to take them, but with everything that had been going on he had to give it some feet.

Lynette perked up a little. B wasn't really a talkative person so the fact that he was zoned in on her conversation motivated her to keep talking. She actually liked the nigga. Maybe this was the beginning of a real relationship.

"...So, yeah, he been spendin' money like it ain't shit. Him an his partna Snake supposedly robbed some Mexicans or something. He said he shot one of them and took a few kilos from they dumb-asses."

Insane's heart started racing. He couldn't believe what he was hearing. Everything she was telling him matched what Mark had described a hundred times since the incident took place.

"... I know he'll give me some cash if I ask."

Insane snatched his phone off the night table and immediately called Mark. "Blood!"

"What's brackin'?"

"Where you at?"

"At the beehive on 12th."

"I'll be there in thirty!"

"'Nuff said."

B put his phone down and turned to Lynette, "Get dressed!"

"For what?" she asked, confused. Had she said something wrong? "Where we going?"

"Ahh, naw, baby. It's good. I just remembered something I needed to holla at the homey 'bout. We just gonna go to blood's spot and smoke for a little while."

"Oh, okay. Let's get some clothes on."

$$\$\$\$\$\$$

Gangsta was outside with some gremlins. They were all posted up under a shade tree on San Jose Way. The

"Way-Way" was a street in the P known for dog fights, dice games and all-around felonious activities. It was one of those days when traffic was high with people coming and going left and right.

About seven F.A.B. niggaz were out there bleeding the block. Their heavy metal was close by, tucked in bushes and an abandoned car or two. It was war time so the goonies were hoping to get an opportunity to use their machinery. Yet, they all knew the chances of someone coming through on a daylight mission was unlikely. The P was hard on outsiders and everyone in Sacramento knew this.

Talton had just stepped away from the crowd to grab a Swisher from his glove compartment when Mark's Mustang pulled up with Insane's Cutlass right behind it. They both parked across the street and stepped out with seroius looks on their faces. Something was up. And Gangsta was prepared for whatever it was.

As soon as he was within earshot, Mark said, "We need to talk."

Gangsta greeted both his comrades with a thugs embrace before replying, "What's brackin', whoop?"

"We got a line on the niggaz that robbed us."

Even before Talton had the chance to fully upload the statement, Insane cut in, "Ol' girl," he motioned towards the female seated in his ride across the street, "got a cousin named Twist. The nigga drives a Van. He been braggin' 'bout robbin' some niggaz. Everything she said matched what happened to y'all."

"Where he from?" Talton asked while glancing towards the Cutlass. *She studying our faces right now*, he thought to himself.

Mark took over; "He from Valley High. You know the nigga, blood. We was at the Boy's Ranch wit' 'im. And, check this out; the nigga the bitch talking 'bout runs with Snake from Valley High."

Talton looked into Mark's eyes. He slowly nodded. They both knew who Snake was. He was one of those niggaz from the South Area who was just as dangerous as they were. "Snake, huh..."

"On Bloods," Mark replied. "It has to be them. I just had this bitch at the house giving me all the intel we need. I know where they layin' they heads at an' all that." M.S. paused when Terauchi and several other young niggaz approached them.

"What's brackin'?" Terauchi asked.

"We got a line on the niggaz that robbed us," Mark answered. "It was some Valley High niggaz."

Rauchi shook his head. "I knew it!"

Q.Q. and May-May, some younger niggaz with Rauchi stopped on their bikes to listen in on their conversation. They were barely in their teens, yet they were just as dangerous as some men twice their age.

"When we gonna slide?" Talton asked in a business-like tone.

"ASAP!" Mark replied.

"What about the bitch?" Talton inquired, glancing towards her once again.

Mark cut his eyes towards Insane before turning back towards Talton. "You already know."

His sinister tone told Gangsta all he needed to know. As he watched Mark and B head back toward their vehicles, he knew wholeheartedly that the girl wouldn't make it through the night. It didn't bother him one bit, either. She had made herself a loose end so her fate was secured by her own doing.

In a way, that thought process right there was why Gangsta hadn't told Mark about Jomara's statements the day he was shot. Any which way he broke it down, she earned a death sentence the moment she opened her mouth to say what she said. But, for some reason Talton had decided to keep that situation to himself.

Terauchi and the other B.G.'s were a few feet from Talton chattering about killing random Valley High niggaz. He could see their thirst for blood. He knew he wouldn't be able to keep them off the front lines even if he wanted to, which he didn't. This was gangland, a world where adolescent gunners were expected to and respected for putting in just as much work as full-grown men.

CHAPTER ELEVEN

TRUE STORY

"The sound of gunfire rivalled that of a 4th of a July celebration."

– King Guru

"Jomara! Jomara! Bein aqui! Ayuda me cosinar esta comida!" Ms. Norma yelled from the kitchen.

Jomara was already on her way in there. She wasn't feeling it, she was under the weather something drastic. "Why is it so hot in here, mami? Damn!"

Her mother took a look at her and immediately saw the condition she was in. Jomara looked sick. She seemed overly fatigued, which her mother couldn't understand why since the girl hadn't left the house in close to two weeks.

"It ain't hot in here! Is you loca or something? Look! The window and the back door is open!"

Suddenly, Jomara felt extremely woozy. The smell of food was nasty. The heat was excruciating. Then, all of a sudden, she felt everything in her stomach coming up to her throat. Jomara covered her mouth and ran to the bathroom. She had to make it to the toilet before she puked all over the house.

Her mother had seen the whole thing. That's when it all started making sense to her. The girl was tired. Her face stayed flushed. Her breast were swollen and she was throwing up. Norma recognized the signs. She'd experienced them herself six times in her life. Norma stepped away from the stove to go to her bedroom to retrieve something she had stashed in one of her bottom drawers. After taking it out she took it to the bathroom. She wanted to rejoice, but knew better than to express her true emotions. It wasn't the proper time nor the place. Instead, she just tossed the box on the floor and said, "Surprised it took this long!" before stepping away as if she didn't care.

Jomara looked up through blurry eyes wondering what the crazy woman was talking about. She felt like shit and didn't have time for her mother's nagging ways. But when she took a look at the item she had tossed on the floor, it all made sense...

A pregnancy test.

$$$$$

"You ready?" Mark asked Insane.

"Damn right!"

M.S. was behind the wheel of a stolen Astro Van carrying a cadre of street marines ready to activate. Their guns were all loaded. Every single one of them cleaned and ready to end lives. In front of the van was a tow truck driven by their older homey, Big K.P. Talton was next to him with murder on his mind as well. The sun had disappeared long before their mission had started. Giving them the perfect cover as they slithered through South Sacramento on their way to Valley High.

The demons from the Mids were dressed for the hunt. Black was the attire for the evening. Black laced with red bandanas to protect their identities while at the same time letting their opps know who they were dealing with. Neither vehicle had its music playing. Half the wolves in this pack were high out of their minds on coke. The nasty drip slowly finding its way down the back of their throats gave them all a certain look of hatred. A look that predators harbored while on the hunt.

When they arrived to the street where they were told Twist lived, they circled the block several times before pulling up to the white and brown house. Under normal circumstances the home would've been as secure as a castle on the top of a mountain. The front door as well as all the home's windows were covered with bars. Tonight, the bars didn't mean shit. They were a minor inconvenience for the determined serial killers set on ending a war in one swoop.

Big K.P. put this tow truck in reverse then drove it onto the grass. Talton was out of its cabin before it stopped. Several of the soldiers who arrived in the Van behind them were out and about as well. Gangsta and Mark quietly took the hook from the back of the tow truck, hooked it up to the security bars protecting the home's front window, then sent a silent message for K.P. to do what needed to be done.

Demons with heavy metal took positions and got ready to blitz. K.P. had the truck in drive and stomped his foot on the gas! Before the tires could gain the necessary traction they destroyed the yard's unkept lawn. Then it took off!

KRSSSHHH! CRRRKKKK! BLAAAM!

The bars ripped from the house. Wood splintered apart. Glass shattered. The destruction was immediate. It was as if the front of the house was ripped right off its foundation.

As soon as the hole was created, the gangland demons swarmed the opened portal. Inside, they found a group of men and women who were so shocked by their entrance that none of them had the chance to defend themselves.

The sound of gunfire rivalled that of a 4th of July celebration. Mark and Talton led the strike. They were the first ones inside. Going through the home like a first-person shooter game.

Twist was found in the bathroom with his pants down. He died with his loaded gun on the counter next to a phone and a bag of weed. Snake wasn't there. Yet, in the end, the hit was considered a success. Seven Valley High Crips were murdered in one move. The whole assault took less than two minutes. They were in and out before the first calls started flooding Sacramento's police department.

And this is how it all started…

To be continued…

$$$$$

DEVILS & DEMONS 1 IS AVAILABLE NOW FROM THE CELL BLOCK AND AMAZON.

PROLOGUE
JUVY

Growing up, I used to think the niggaz with the big names in the hood were like Gods. You know, like how them Italian motherfuckers labeled each other "made men." But when you're young and caught up in the visual aspect of shit, it's easy to lose sight of the real. You get deceived by all the smoke and mirrors, and I had no idea of the depths I was to fall. I'd fallen so far from reality that I found myself staring at my reflection and had no idea it was me. I'd found the pits of death. It was filled with burning souls, screaming as the trapped walls were starting to collapse. Everything was burning around me. It was inevitable. You know, dealing with the death culture of the streets and what came along with such a lifestyle.

The fortunate elect to gamble because they're in a position to sustain a loss. So, if you're not amongst the fortunate, then maybe gambling isn't conducive to your survival. But of course, niggaz don't think like that. Everything is a hustle. I'm not writing this to make it seem as if I'm this bigger-than-life kind of nigga, or like I'm one hell of a dude. Nawl. I'm just an average Joe. But the one thing that separates me from most niggaz dwelling in the slums is my willingness to sacrifice and take whatever measures are needed to get shit done.

See, I came up around all sorts of people that played the game. Dope fiends who know how to rob. Crack heads who broke into shit and stole the entire house chasing a high. Killers that got away with murder. And even grimy-ass niggaz that played outside the rules of decency. So naturally, at the age of just 19 years old, I've seen some shit.

I try to stay within the lines that are governed by the respected. I had no brothers growing up. My pops was a piece of shit and my mother smoked crack. All I knew was the struggle. I would sit back and watch the older guys in the hood and study gangster flicks. That was a real thing for me. That was the school I chose to learn from in order to perfect my craft. Honestly though, I was stuck in two different worlds trying to figure out who I was. That is the world that so many like myself come from. I guess that's why it's called the death culture...

Chicago, Illinois
Southside

"You have to think outside the box, look at everything and leave no stone unturned," said Paul. We all have a choice, and if that choice leaves behind a trail of destruction, then that blood is on the hands of the man that initiated it. You see, we have two animals that reside within us. The one you feed the most, well, that's the one that'll survive."

"I get the logic, but it's pointless for me to sit here with you and listen to philosophy. This is going to happen," said Juvy.

"Yeah, sure it is. But ask yourself one last thing: Why you?" Paul inquired.

"I don't really ask questions – not my thing. They place an order, I deliver," Young Juvy replied and looked at the older man with a stale expression.

"The culture has shifted, but that's a talk for another time. If I were you, I'd take note of this day and hold on to it. There will always be more storms to come. I'm sure of it. You do what you have to do."

Paul got up, walked to the window and took a seat in a rocking chair. He began to hum an old tune that put his mind at rest. He wasn't naive. He knew this day would come. Juvy approached him and pointed the gun at the back of his head.

Humming.

"Just remember this day."

"These are the days that always stick around no matter how much you try to let them go," Juvy said, and pulled the trigger.

The first shot crashed into the back of Paul's skull and put his brains on the window. The second shot put him in a permanent sleep.

When Juvy made it to the awaiting car in the alley a few blocks over, Flukey pulled off once he got inside.

Although this was part of the game, he still knew something about it wasn't right. There were questions eating away at his conscience. Paul was what you considered to be a made man. He was like royalty in the Black Disciple organization. Why kill your own

Dynasty member? Most importantly, why him? These were the questions running rapidly through Juvy's head.

Paul was the last of the last. There weren't any others like him around.

Most of them were either dead or doing life in a prison cell. Now that Paul was out of the picture, things were definitely about to change.

"Did you make sure h –"

"The nigga dead," Juvy said before Flukey could even finish his sentence.

Flukey was teaching him the game. They were like brothers and Juvy respected him more than anyone else. Flukey was a gangster and was feared amongst many. He took a liking to Juvy and pulled him under his wing. Being that Juvy didn't have a father figure nor any brothers, he filled that void.

"Give me the blick." Flukey wanted the gun so he could get rid of it.

Juvy passed it to him and he gave it to Crazy. Juvy didn't really know Crazy. Mainly because he'd done a stretch in the joint. Both Juvy and Crazy locked eyes through the rear-view mirror. He was a lot older than both him and Flukey. Crazy had a reputation for putting in work for the guys, but none of that shit mattered to Juvy. There was something about him that rubbed Juvy the wrong way and he couldn't let it go.

Flukey pulled over and Crazy jumped out of the car. He approached the bridge and tossed the gun into the river. He pulled the hood up over his head and got back into the car.

"You did good, lil bro, but this doesn't leave this car," Flukey instructed Juvy.

"Say less. I got'chu," he replied. This only added to the mystery and perplexity circling around in his young mind. There was always secrecy and hidden agendas. This was the part of the game he had a hard time grasping.

"I got to drop you off real quick. We need to handle something," Flukey informed him.

Juvy was cool with that. Besides, he needed some time to himself.

The ride back to the house seemed off and distant. It was different this time. Juvy closed his eyes and allowed his mind to shift – to dwell in a different realm than reality. But he couldn't get Paul's words out of his head.

Juvy was in a sunken place, remembering the meaningful gaze in Paul's eyes. There was a look of familiarity that stuck with him from their very first introduction. Juvy felt connected to him. As if the two shared a familiar story.

At times it seemed as if he was trying to warn him about something. The game was cold and filled with so many disappointments, but he knew what he'd signed up for.

Juvy opened his eyes the moment Flukey pulled into the driveway. He opened the car door and shut it behind him.

"Juvy, come here for a second, lil bro," Flukey called him back to the car.

"Wussup?"

"You seem like your mind is somewhere else. You good?"

"Yeah, I'm straight."

"I'm just making sure you good. I'll holla at'chu once I get back," Flukey assured him.

"Fa'sho!"

With that, he walked off and went inside the house.

Spilling blood is the easy part, cleaning it up is the trick...!

CHAPTER 1

FLUKEY

Flukey picked Juvy up from the spot and headed towards the expressway. Crazy sat in the back seat. He loaded one of the guns and passed it to Juvy. He had gotten used to going on missions for the Mob, it was just another day at the office for him. Flukey liked having Juvy put in work because he never asked questions. Most importantly, if things were to go south, he knew Juvy wouldn't roll and talk to the pigs. Juvy was willing to follow Flukey no matter where it led him. Flukey was a good nigga, and for that alone, Juvy vowed to accept his leadership. Crazy? Well that was another story. This had to be something serious. Crazy never came with them, and Juvy felt different about this ride. Something was in the air.

"I'm about to ask you to do something, and I need you to make sure it's taken care of. Juvy, make sure you handle this – no mistakes," Flukey explained.

"I got it. Who am I hitting?"

"P. You gotta hit P."

"P – as in Paul – *our* P?" Juvy was flabbergasted with perplexity.

P was the man. He was high-ranking Black Disciple and a somebody. Niggaz like him don't just get killed, but when they do, there's always a motive behind it. P called the plays. Nothing happened on the streets without him knowing. Juvy knew these things and that alone threw him for a loop. How could a nigga with power like P get twisted up like this?

"This come from the old man," Flukey assured him.

He was referring to King Von, who was the highest ranked Black Disciple in the Mob. He was crowned Supreme Board Member by BJ himself, which was why he got the name King Von. The unique thing about him, although he was a righteous dude, was the nigga was serving a life sentence for murder in Stateville Correctional Center.

This was the first time that Juvy had ever questioned Flukey, but it was fair judgment. His gut told him to walk away from this hit, but the streets didn't allow you to pick and choose. This was a call coming from the top, and now wasn't the time to be second guessing himself. Juvy felt like the joints had too much power over the streets. *How the fuck you let a nigga doing life in prison control what goes on in the free world?* At least that's how he thought.

"Consider it done," Juvy said, and Flukey just remained silent.

Flukey's head was filled with questions too, but just like his young protege, he didn't ask questions either. Flukey and P were extremely close, so to be asked to take him out – shit was foul. But the game didn't operate off of feelings, nor was it dictated by "big I's and small you's." The business was the business, law governed all events, and this was an event set to change the course of the Mob forever.

There were layers to reaching a certain height in this game. Most niggaz who climb the ladder of success, got it done by getting their hands dirty. It was the nature of the culture. While Flukey was going over things in his head trying to make sense out of a play of this magnitude, Crazy smacked Juvy's seat.

"What'chu scared, lil' nigga?"

Juvy didn't bother to reply. He gave him a look that indicated otherwise.

"He good, this not his first rodeo," Flukey shot back.

"I think the lil' nigga might not be up for this one tho'." Crazy kept poking.

"Yo, you talk too much. Flukey, pull over right here," Juvy added, and Flukey obliged.

"Why am I pulling over?"

"There's a camera when you hit the main street and a couple more in the alley. I don't want to be seen getting out of the car. Meet me on the next block from his spot in the alley."

Juvy pulled on his hood and turned to face Crazy.

"I knew what I signed up for a long time ago. All that scared shit you're talking – wrong dude," he said and got out of the car.

"You think he'll get it done?" Crazy asked Flukey.

"Without a doubt. Shorty's thorough and more than capable of handling shit like this." Flukey was sure of him and Crazy just sat back and waited to see what would happen.

It wasn't the same – the game, that is. There was no honor amongst the respected and there were new rules. Ones that forbid the old law. Niggaz were crabs in a barrel. Once you managed to get a leg out, a motherfucker would pull you back down and leave you plotting to get to the top again. This was the game. Sometimes you win, sometimes you don't.

Crazy had just been released from prison. He'd done a stretch back-to-back. Now that he was a free man, his intentions seemed a bit out of the sorts. Flukey knew he was bad news, but if a call came down from the top, he had to oblige.

"If this came from King Von, why wouldn't he send word through the proper chain?" Flukey questioned.

"Because, this was on the need-to-know basis. He didn't want it to leak out and then Paul be on point for someone to make a move. Plus, I was on my way out the door and he wanted me to personally deliver the message," explained Crazy.

"Right."

That was all Flukey had to say. It still seemed a bit suspicious.

"Where do you know this kid from?"

"You seem stuck on him for some reason. Why?" Flukey felt as if Crazy was threatened by Juvy somehow.

"I make it my business to thoroughly understand all those around me. We're tied to him now. I just passed him a gun and you just gave him an order to kill someone, so any liabilities is a grave concern to me. I'm not going back to prison. My next trip there will put me away for the rest of my life."

Crazy made sense of it, Flukey just wasn't trying to hear it. He knew Juvy too well and trusted him with his own life.

"Juvy good." Flukey dismissed the conversation and waited for his young protege to emerge.

"What if he misses?"

Crazy just couldn't let it go, and it was starting to irritate Flukey.

"Crazy, he got this. Let him work. Once he make it back to the car, take the gun and get rid of it in the river. But right now isn't the time to be questioning a nigga that's already on the hit."

"I'm covering our ass, and if you have a problem with it, oh well. I just think we should have had a backup plan in case the lil' nigga misses."

"He don't miss. Never has."

As Flukey was explaining things to Crazy, Juvy emerged from the side of a house and got inside the car.

"Did you make sure h –"

"The nigga dead."

A FEW MONTHS EARLIER...

Stateville Correctional Center

Prison is a world trapped inside of another world, but this one in particular is a gateway between the streets and niggaz isolated from society. The methodical and strategic type of niggaz, they use prison to analyze and process information, then build bridges with important people that connect agendas in retrospect to the hustle. How do you think official niggaz such as Larry Hoover, King Shorty, Bo Didly, and other high-ranking chiefs built their empires? They forged bridges behind prison walls.

Niggaz in prison are always the first to know when some shit done hit the fan or when a nigga get put on ice. Shit like that becomes first-hand knowledge for key figures in prison. Why? Because you can't run shit without knowing what's being done on the streets.

There're layers to the top. A chain of command. The in-between niggaz take orders from a ghost – that means they'll never be in the same room as the nigga calling the plays. In the streets, that's what's called an authority figure.

Gang Chiefs are appointed. They're the motherfuckers with the real power who orchestrate shit on a higher level. Those niggaz, you don't really bump into. They don't make themselves available for conversation. At the end of the day, it's about money, but within the ranks of any Mob it's about power, because the nigga that controls shit is the nigga that collects.

See, Chicago, besides it being cold as fuck, has always been a city controlled by gangsters. Motherfuckers like Al Capone and other Italian mobsters. But now, the tables have turned, and smaller factions, like the Black Disciples, have been granted dominion. Don't take this as no biased shit, just because it's being told from the prospective of a Born Divine; but then again, you might be right.

The gangsters, though, them motherfuckers aren't going anywhere. They're enriched in Chicago's culture. On the southside, there's mostly Disciples. Out west, not so much. That's more of a melting pot with different factions of Vicelords and Four Corner Hustlers. Each a powerhouse and force to be reckoned with in their own right.

Every Mob is pushing shit around throughout the neighborhoods in Chicago, so it makes sense for the top chiefs to have open lines of communication to find solutions and resolve disputes. You can't war and get money at the same time. Shit don't really work like that. But the key to it all is the fucking Mexicans. Those are the motherfuckers with the means to get you rich, and I ain't talking about just being able to flip whips kind of money. They're supplying the entire city. Flooding the streets with everything you could possibly think of. But here we are, trying to kill each other off to profit more than the next man. I mean, it's a jungle – fuck you expect?

Stateville houses everyone from rapists and drug dealers, to serial killers. It also houses some of the most violent and disruptive inmates in the state. When you're isolated from society for so long, and left with nothing but time to think, you find ways to make the very things deemed impossible, possible. Impossible shit like running a fully functioning criminal enterprise from a prison cell.

Wars amongst rival gangs is to be expected, but the real conflicts seem to always be internal. You have those in power on the streets doing their thing, then there are those with death sentences dictating shit from inside. That's where things become hazardous, extremely problematic and dangerous.

"I need to holla at Von," Crazy told one of the guys that stood watch near his cell.

King Von had been groomed and taught by King BJ. The thing about BJ was that he wasn't like most Kings. He was well-spoken and reserved. He didn't have a problem admitting when he was wrong about

93

something. Most importantly, he accepted his penalties for any and every transgression placed by his actions. But of course, no one in their right mind was foolish enough to bring the King up on charges. I'm saying all of this to say he wasn't one of those leaders blinded by power, nor did he allow his stature to cloud his ability to think.

Crazy was on his way out the door. He wanted to come home and position himself to make a substantial move. One that would solidify his standings within the Mob. History wasn't in his favor, though. He was one of those crab-type niggaz that wanted to be high in authority, but every time he climbed the ladder of success, prison plagued his chances and sabotaged the path before him. Sadly, that was being written in the history books.

"I understand you've been trying to have a sit-down with me for quite some time now," King Von said the minute Crazy stepped into his cell.

"As you know, I'm on my way out the door, and I need to get my feet wet. You know, I need your blessing to jump into the swing of things."

"What are you asking exactly?"

"I got my own men, and they're willing to follow me wherever. I just need a piece of land to call mine, and not have to answer to anyone."

"How long have you been gone?"

"Almost fifteen years," Crazy replied.

"And you sure you want to get involved with what's going on in them streets?"

"I've already sacrificed a great deal of my life for the Mob. I'm all in."

"I don't cross boundaries, and to say I support you taking a piece of land away from them young guys that have been fighting to keep it grounded, well, that wouldn't be fair to them. Besides, there's a Board. The Board runs the streets and I let them do their own thing."

"I can deal with a Board. I just need a way in." Crazy wanted to get involved and potentially eradicate them at the top to take his position. It was personal for him. He had a hidden agenda and a score to settle.

"I can't guarantee you a spot on the Board, but I can look into something else," King Von explained.

"Look, I know you and Paul have an unsettled –"

"Let me stop you right there. What's going on between myself and P, that's between the two of us. It's none of your business. If that's the wild card you're banking on using to get into the mix of things, you're barking up the wrong tree."

King Von quickly took offense.

"Pardon me if I stepped out of bounds, but Paul is losing members that are willing to follow him. I know how to lead and keep shit afloat. On top of that –"

Crazy looked around and leaned forward. Whatever he whispered into King Von's ear caught his attention.

"Now you need to be sure of what you're saying. Be very careful of your tongue," warned the King.

"I stand behind my words!" Crazy assured him.

King Von studied him for any sign of deception. This was something extremely out of left field and downright foul.

"How do you know this is true?"

"Because I was the one who saw it through. He gave me the order."

Crazy knew this would either go his way or get him killed, but it was a risk worth taking. King Von stood to his feet and told the men in the room to leave. What he had to say to Crazy needed to be said in private.

"I've always figured he had something to do with what happened that day. Karma's a bitch. Listen, you take my word to the streets with you and I'll be sure to make room for you on the Board after you take care of Paul."

As King Von and Crazy spoke, Yatta sat outside the cell and caught bits and pieces of what was being said. He never trusted Crazy. The nigga was grimy and shouldn't be trusted. Being that Yatta was from Buff City and Paul was their appointed chief, he had his ears open to what was being said.

Paul and King Von had been at odds for nearly two decades, and their feud had yet to find a conclusion. King Von was sentenced to forever and a day in prison. To keep the peace and the Mob from splitting into two sects, King Von decided to keep his beef with Paul away from the functioning of their organization. Although he was their King, he understood the importance of having other authority figures.

Paul wasn't just the highest ranked member on the streets; he was also King Von's brother. The brotherly beef between the two men started after Trina got killed. King Von knew at the time of her death that Paul wasn't ready to face prison, so he took the ride and gave the organization to his brother to lead.

That's when the betrayal began to unfold. But Crazy had just dropped a bomb and now it went from old beef to a current war to be fought on all fronts.

CHAPTER 2
JUVY

He ran as fire burned in his lungs from exhaustion. He was taking long tiresome strides as bullets pursued his trail, ricocheting with ill intentions to carry his soul across the threshold of death.

Juvy knew death would find him eventually. He'd already made peace with himself about it if that day happened to find him sooner rather than later. Of course, the game was cold, but that was the fare it cost to play.

He returned fire but it was in vain. There was too many of them. This was it. That awful gut feeling of defeat turned in his stomach and fought against his hope – the little bit of hope that kept his legs moving. The crazy part about it all was that Juvy didn't budge emotionally. In fact, there was a sense of relief. He would finally be able to rest and not have to look over his shoulders every day. But that didn't mean he would just lay down and be consumed by his assailants.

It was never fun when you were the one on the other end of the gun, being hunted by a man who anticipated pulling the trigger. Although Juvy was only a kid, the streets didn't differentiate between adolescents and grown men. There was no in-between. Juvy's legs gave out from the exhaustion, so he rolled underneath a parked van and prepared himself for the worst. He waited. His body and mind calm, ready for whatever was to come. Again, fear wasn't what surfaced. His mind traveled to an empty place. Then, he thought about where his soul would go. He wasn't religious, nor had he ever thought about God, but what if all the stories were true? You know, the whole heaven and hell thing. If God were to judge him for the deeds he'd done thus far; shid, he had a one-way trip to hell on a propane tank.

Juvy heard footsteps near the van. Hopefully they would keep going, but luck had never found his side of circumstances. It wasn't a thing for him.

Juvy only had a few rounds left, and he counted at least six men that were pursuing him. The cold metal he gripped in his palm kept his nerves in check. One thing for sure, he wouldn't go down without a fight. Dying wasn't the hard part. Having to deal with the mess you left behind was the thing.

"He stopped right here – I swear," said one of the men.

They started to search the area, and before he could brace himself for a possible gun fight, someone grabbed hold of his foot and pulled him from underneath the van. He tried to get a shot off, but another one of the men kicked the gun from his hand. They surrounded him and started kicking the shit out of him while yelling slurs of anger. In the midst of so many people trying to get a kick in, Juvy managed to get to his feet. At this point, dying was inevitable. He would just rather die on his feet than go out on his back.

Juvy threw a punch and was instantly swarmed and sent back to the ground. A shot rang out and everybody stopped. Juvy held his stomach and blood filled his hand. Another shot crashed into his chest and blood spilled from his mouth. As he struggled to breathe, something strange and serene happened. Everybody standing around him disappeared and the pitch-black sky was replaced with an ambient stream of radiant beams and a vibrant blue sky. Juvy readied for the sky, hoping God would at least forgive him for all the wrong he'd done, overlook his transgressions and accept him into the golden pastures of the afterlife. He closed his eyes and smiled.

One of the men approached him and placed a gun barrel to his head. Still, there was no fear nor plea for mercy, just a desolate gaze of utter emptiness. The man pulled the trigger and the muzzle flash was followed by a loud buzzing from Juvy's alarm clock. He opened his eyes and just laid there for a moment. The morning sun light came through the partially opened blinds and caused him to shift positions. He often had these kind of dreams – dreams about how he would die. At first, they were startling, but eventually they became routine. Hell, if you swim in shit for so long, you'll get used to it. That's what sparked the thoughts in his mind about there being a God. You know, if he was real and all. But coming from the streets and playing in the gravel of the death culture, motherfuckers didn't put too much thought into there being a God. Besides, he didn't do shit for niggaz playing the game anyway.

When Juvy walked into the kitchen, he found some of the guys at the table. The tension in the air was apparent, and Juvy knew something big had transpired. Premo and Double looked as if they were ready to lose it. Premo had a reputation for being problematic, and most of the niggaz in the hood didn't fuck around with him. There were so many people in the kitchen that it looked like they were having a session.

"What's up? What's going on?" Juvy asked.

"P dead. Niggaz clapped him," Lil Chris said as be fought back tears.

Lil Chris was a good nigga. He was also Flukey's older brother, just built different.

"This shit not gon' rest until we find out who's responsible," added Premo.

Juvy just sat back and listened as they vented their frustrations. Flukey and Crazy were nowhere to be found. It was as if Juvy was left to shoulder the awkward tension of knowing exactly what happened to Paul.

"Who killed him?" Juvy asked, hoping to sound concerned.

"Muthafuckas don't know shit, and that's the fuckin' problem," Double said and punched the wall.

"I'ma hit Flukey and see where he at." Juvy made an attempt to leave the kitchen, but the guys advised him to keep quiet about what was going on – at least to stay off the phone with it.

This wasn't good, and he knew the Mob wasn't going to let it go. Juvy just didn't understand the secrecy amongst the multitude. How could you call the guys your brothers, but keep something of this magnitude away from them? Juvy grabbed his hoodie.

"I'm about to hit the streets and see what's being

said. If Flukey comes looking for me, let him know I'm out and about," he informed them, then took off.

Juvy leaned his head against the window as the bus drove up the street. He had no idea where he was headed. Running the streets and dealing with the Mob was becoming a problem for him. The more he saw what went on behind closed doors and all the snake shit niggaz did for power, the more it made him want out. Maybe God was real, and he was trying to reach out and tell him something before it was too late. Juvy had a lot of questions and the answers seemed to be miles apart from the void in his desperate need for fulfillment. Life wasn't promised, and at the rate he was moving, he was basically living on borrowed time.

Juvy looked up and peered out the window. He noticed a massive church on the corner. Before the bus could pull off from the light, he quickly pulled the stop cord to notify the driver to pull over. Juvy had no idea what he was doing, but he got off the bus and headed towards the church. As he climbed the steps to the entrance, he forgot something. He was strapped. He quickly went to stash his gun, then walked into the church. There was nobody inside. It was massive and had all sorts of religious paintings and statues everywhere. He walked towards the sound of a piano playing on the other side of the building. Upon turning the corner, he ran into a huge statue. It was a depiction of Jesus Christ. Only this one was different from the others he was used to seeing around the hood. It was a black Jesus. Juvy was so caught up in the fine craftsmanship that he didn't notice the man standing next to him until he spoke.

"Did you know Jesus died for our sins? He died so we can have the free will that we have today."

Juvy turned and saw an older gentleman. To his surprise, they appeared to have similar features. For the most part, he looked nothing like a preacher. "Wasn't he like, God's son, or some shit like that?"

"Yeah, he was. For God so loved the world that he sent his only son to suffer for us."

"That dont make sense tho' – fuck would he do some shit like that? I get lost when trying to rationalize the logic behind a lot of this religious shit."

"It didn't make any sense to me neither, but in time, you'll understand. You just have to open your heart and let him in."

"God has never done anything for me or my people, so it's hard to just up and believe in a ghost," Juvy replied, and the man laughed.

"You remind me of myself, but it'll all come to you in due time. I've never seen you around here before..."

"Yeah, I'm from the Southside. I wanted to come in and try to figure out a few things in my life."

"Well, you're in the right place. What's your name?"

"My name Juvy!"

"Alright then, Juvy, nice to meet you. My name is Brother James."

"I don't know a lot about the God thing, but I'm willing to give it a shot."

"That's all it takes. Whether you believe this or not, God sent you here for a reason. You just have to stick around long enough to figure out why."

"So, where do we start?" Juvy really wanted to give this a shot. He hoped to find himself while on this journey. For his entire life he'd always allowed people to control him and use him for their own selfish reasons. Now he had to take the time to help himself. All he knew was destruction, chaos and more chaos. Life had its challenges, and he knew them all too well.

"We start with this." James pointed to his chest, then continued. "You start with your heart. You have to choose God, because you can't serve two masters. You'll grow to love one and despise the other."

As he listened to him speak, Juvy started to really question a lot of things. He wasn't sure what he wanted for himself. He just knew he didn't want to die young in the streets. The world he came from had conditioned him to live for the moment with the understanding that tomorrow wasn't promised to no one. The game was rigged. There wasn't any winners or losers. Just idle time being consumed by empty voids. It's like a cycle of never-ending tyranny.

Brother James sat him down and went over a few scriptures. The more he talked, the more it drew Juvy in and made him think.

"If God loves us so much, why he let babies and shit get shot?"

"We can't question why God allows certain things to happen. He operates on his own time. I used to ask those same questions until I decided to just give in and trust him. My faith grew and drove me closer to his divinity."

"I gotta work on that," Juvy replied with a chuckle.

"Sure you do. I have to start preparing for my class. You're more than welcome to stay and get the word."

"I think I'll sit this one out – baby steps, my dude." Juvy smiled and gave him some dap.

He stood to leave, and in that instance, he knew the place he was headed back to wasn't ideal. It was a pit. A burning pit consumed by fire and debris. Brother James grabbed him by the shoulders and looked him in the eyes.

"Save yourself before it's too late. There's still time. There's still hope.

"You have a darkness in your eyes that I know. One that nearly consumed me. That war you have going on within, I fought it too. But you have to chose a side."

"I don't know how to do that. It's like I'm trapped," Juvy admitted.

Brother James felt his sincerity and it moved him. He wanted to help him before it was too late.

"Dig deeper. You have to fight on the side of the light. Stay away from the darkness."

"I'm trying."

"Try harder. Fight harder!"

He really had his attention now and Juvy felt something for the first time in young life. He felt like someone really cared about him and wasn't just using him for their own selfish reasons.

"What if I can't?"

"All you have to do is focus on the light. The fight is between the two. Good and bad. You're just the vessel being used. You must choose a side. That's important in this journey, because if not, they'll implode and take you with them."

Juvy saw a certain level of sincerity in his eyes and felt that his plea was genuine. He had nothing to say in return. It was something he had no answer for. When he made it to the door, he stopped and turned around.

"You think I can come back sometime?"

"The door is always open."

Carnage-filled neighborhoods are always the wrath of men. Writings on the wall that are inked in blood from the destruction of chaos left behind. All due to the absence of God...

$$$$$

Stank was causing a lot of problems for the BD's, and being that his name was ringing as the go-to authority figure for the GD's, he caught the attention of the wrong people. We all know how this goes. Everybody is going to die – some you just have to kill...

There was a bunch of guys shooting dice in the alley right off 118th Place and Indiana. The BD's stronghold was up the hill. They called it BUFF CITY. They had all the blocks from 118th and State to 120th and Yale – some in-between streets as well. Their feud was with the GD's and the Four Corner Hustlers. The Hunits (hundreds) were wild. Bodies were dropping every few hours, or at least motherfuckers were getting shot. It was a war zone with no signs of the violence subsiding.

"Point seven, nigga. Put up or shut up," Burger said as he grabbed the dice.

"I got'chu – shoot!" Boogie replied.

This was the norm. Niggaz hustled and shot dice. While this was going on, no one noticed the two men in hoodies come through the gangway. Before the dice came to a complete stop, shots rang out.

BOOM!

BOOM!

BOOM!

BOOM!

They scattered about, tripping over each other in desperation to avoid the hot metal being dispersed from the two smoking guns. Juvy chased one of them around a house and hit him twice in the back. Crazy shot ferociously and caught another one trying to duck around a vehicle.

BOOM!

BOOM!

BOOM!

Stank returned fire, nearly catching Juvy before he ducked for cover. The trio exchanged gunfire as police sirens could be heard in the distance. Juvy tried to hold his position but Stank had the upper hand. The police sirens were growing closer. They all ran and made a dashing escape before it was too late.

"Fuck!" Crazy yelled, and punched the dash board of the car out of frustration. He was mad that he couldn't kill the nigga he wanted most – Stank. "I had that nigga," he added.

Premo was driving. He was another one of the guys that Juvy knew all too well. Premo had been putting in work for the Mob for as long as he could remember. Juvy looked up to him and considered him to be a big brother. Premo was a part of the reason he started coming up the hill. Juvy was originally from The Dirty Block, which was 119th and Prairie.

"Lil bro, you good?" Premo asked Juvy.

"Yeah," he replied as police cars raced past them.

"Hold up for a sec," Juvy said, and started looking towards one of the alleys. "Let me out."

Premo stopped the car. Juvy took off towards the alley. Apparently, something had caught his attention. He ducked behind one of the garbage cans and waited. He spotted a guy named Smoke, who was one of their rivals. Smoke was coming out of a house and walking to his car. Once he got close enough, Juvy sprang from his position.

BOOM!

The first shot went through his hand as Smoke tried to cover his face. Juvy shot him again in the chest, and once more in the face. Premo pulled down the alley and picked him up. And just like that, another body was added to the gun violence in Chicago.

It always amazed him how niggaz could go take a life, then come back to the trap and party like nothing happened. Juvy was in his room sitting in the dark. For some reason the conversation he had with Brother James was on the forefront of his thoughts. Although he'd just killed somebody, he wasn't fazed. It was the nature of the jungle. It was kill or be killed. Truthfully though, he was starting to scare himself. Mainly because he didn't feel anything. Taking another man's life should make you feel like shit.

The first person he'd ever shot was a crackhead

named Phil. Phil tried to play him and take his work, so Juvy pulled out a .38 Special and pointed it at him. Phil must have thought he was scared to use it, because he laughed and tried to walk off. Juvy pulled the trigger and shot him in the leg then ran off. He was sure he'd killed him until Phil was spotted a few days later wearing a cast.

Juvy never considered himself to be a killer, he just knew if it ever came down to it, he would kill someone. Paul once told him that there were two types of killers in this world. One that would kill to survive, and other that would kill for sport. Kids, women – it didn't matter.

Killing Paul was the worst he'd ever felt about anything. When you choose this life, you're choosing to follow orders, and that's whether you like them or not. Juvy saw something in Paul's gaze that seemed so familiar upon their first introduction. It was like he knew him.

While consumed in his thoughts, his phone rang. When he answered, it was an automated voice system inquiring if he would accept the charges from an inmate at Stateville Correctional Center. Juvy was confused and a bit perplexed. Who would be calling him from prison? He accepted the charges.

"Who is this?"

"My name Yatta. We play for the same team. Hopefully you understand what that mean without me having to dig deeper."

"I get what it mean. Why you calling me tho'?"

"Because I think you need to know who I am."

"And why is that?"

"To keep you from playing out of bounds. Plus, I knew your father."

The line went quiet.

"You there?" Yatta asked.

"Fuck you know about my father?"

"We sat at the table together, and that's all I'm willing to indulge over this phone. If you want some answers, you got to sit across the table from me, and we'll have this dialogue in person."

"With all due respect to you – fuck that nigga. He ain't done shit for me in all this time, I don't need to know him."

"That's cool. Besides, getting to know him now isn't possible. The nigga dead. When you're willing to put your pride to the side and figure out what's really going on within yo' own circle, come holla at me," Yatta said, then ended the call.

Juvy was confused. What the fuck was he talking about? The call was so random and unexpected. He knew nothing about his father and he wanted to keep it like that, but Yatta mentioning something going on within his clique had caught him off guard even more. Something wasn't right. Ever since Crazy had popped up on the scene, a lot of shit was turning sour.

CHAPTER 3

CRAZY

Crazy jumped the gate and moved cautiously along the side of the house. He had sat in his cell and thought about this very day so many times. He had fantasized about getting even with everyone that crossed him. It was one thing to sit in prison for some shit you actually committed, but it was something entirely different to do time as an innocent man. Of course, he had some hidden agendas nobody knew about, but who didn't? But now it was all about him and only him. He was done sacrificing for the Mob.

He made it to the back door of the house and checked the lock – nothing. After looking around for another way in, he noticed that the basement window was slightly open. It took no time to get inside the house. Crazy pulled his gun out and proceeded up the stairs. Nothing had changed much inside the house, just that the air smelled different. He knew his way through the home because at a point in his past it had belonged to him.

The wee hours of the night always seemed eerie and out of place to him. Crazy knew how to play the game, and sometimes that meant getting your hands dirty. His heart was cold and capable of crossing whatever line deemed necessary to get ahead.

When he made it to the kitchen, he ran into a familiar thought. A thought of when he was in love with the very woman he was paying a visit to. She used to greet him with hot hot meals and cool morning kisses on his way out the door. But that wasn't a real thing anymore.

Crazy made it to her bedroom and opened the door. She was sleeping. He took a seat in the chair next to the bed and stared at her for a moment. She was sleeping peacefully and undisturbed, at least until he turned the bedside lamp on.

Gwen opened her eyes and struggled for a moment to adjust to the bright light. When she saw it was Crazy, she immediately sat up and put her back to the headboard.

"What are you doing in my house?"

"I think we're well past that. You crossed me and I want to know why?"

"Well, if you're looking for answers, I'm the wrong person to give 'em to you. I'm not the one who put you in prison, so if you're here to kill me, do what the fuck you got to do."

"You always were fearless – I taught you that. I gave you a good life and took care of you. Yet, you still chose the other side. You thought I wouldn't find out – bad judgment call."

"I have no idea what you're talking about." Gwen reached for a cigarette.

"You think I'm here by accident?"

"I don't give a fuck why you're here," she shot back, and lit the cigarette.

"What did Paul get you into?"

112

"Oh, that's what this is all about? You're mad and pissed on some jealous shit. Paul wasn't a thing for me, it just sort of happened."

"Maybe you can't give me the answers I'm looking for after all."

"BINGO!" Gwen said, and blew a heap of smoke into his face. "You can't kill me. I don't care how mad you are, you can't cross that line."

"Yeah, I know," Crazy said, and pointed the gun at her head, then pulled the trigger. She died instantly.

After watching the life slowly drain from her body, he went into the kitchen. Crazy turned on the stove and snatched the gas line from out the wall. He left out the back door just as the house went up in flames. Although he loved her with everything inside of him, it had to be done and he had to be the one to do it. She had violated and broke his trust in the worst way when she wore a wire and put a tracker on his car. Subsequently, he was convicted of murder and sentenced to life in prison. Luckily, his lawyers were able to find enough newly discovered evidence to exonerate him, and the conviction was overturned.

Crazy felt as if the Mob belonged to him. He had taken a fall and sacrificed too much. Not to mention he felt he had been betrayed by his own brothers in the process.

$$$$$

Juvy was on the porch when Crazy pulled up to the spot. There wasn't much between the two of them. Juvy was always standoffish, and Crazy could sense that he didn't care too much for him.

"You don't like me, do you?" Crazy asked as he walked up.

"What?" Juvy was taken aback by the line of questioning.

"I can tell you're not feeling me, and that's cool, but know that I put on for the guys. I've sacrificed a lot for this thang, and I'm cool with not being the good guy."

"I don't give a fuck about all that, and I don't know you well enough to dislike you. I got my own shit going on."

"So what's your story? Where did you come from?"

"My story is the same as everyone else's. I come from no place special," Juvy replied.

Crazy laughed.

"I've heard a lot about'chu – great things. I was told you put a'lotta work in for the Mob. I used to be that guy, but times have changed. I respect the gangstas – true indeed. But more so than others, I respect the niggaz that laid the bricks of the foundation we stand on today. The niggaz who are set to die in prison for their sacrifices that enable you to call yourself a Black Disciple today. Them niggaz I respect even more than money," Crazy explained.

"What's the point of this conversation?"

"I'm not against you. You can trust me."

"Trust is a strong word, but I got'chu, big dawg," Juvy said, and pushed past Crazy as if he wasn't nothing.

Crazy watched the youngin stroll off as he stood there feeling disrespected. While in his thoughts, his phone rang.

"I found it."

"Bet 'em up. Make sure you're careful putting it at the drop," Crazy informed the person on the line.

"Got it. It was cold as fuck, but luckily you threw it where I could easily find it," said the voice on the phone.

"I got to go. Make sure all the people on your end know what needs to be done."

Crazy ended the call and went inside the spot. Shit was coming together better than he had anticipated.

$$$$$

FLUKEY

The city of Chicago has always been known for violence, but now shit had went from bad to worse. The Hunits were wild, and Buff City was the focal point for the majority of the shootings and homicides in the city. That made it much harder to hustle and get money.

Flukey was only 37 years old, but in the streets, shid, that's a lifetime. When the hood's namesake, Big Buff, was still alive, things were different and most of the guys were in compliance with the rule of law. However, this was the life that had chose Flukey, and he accepted it. He would die a street nigga. Nothing more, nothing less.

Although the call made on Paul had come from the top, Flukey was still skeptical and he wanted to see what was to it. They had killed a good nigga, but there was no taking sides when plays like that were called. Flukey just needed to be sure.

After putting a flame to his blunt, he called Clee. Clee was one of the guys, but he didn't really fuck with the multitude. He kind of stayed to himself. If anyone had the answers he was looking for, it would start with him.

"Wassup, broski?" Clee answered.

"I can't call it. I'm taking it one day at a time."

"You got to. How the nigga Crazy holding up?"

"He good."

"Tell him I send my regards. I know that shit fucked him up. On top of that –"

"Wait, what'chu talkin 'bout?" Flukey was confused.

"Gwen!"

"What about Gwen?"

"You ain't heard? They found her dead and the crib was burned down," Clee informed him.

"Damn." That was all he could say.

"Any word on that P situation?"

"We're still on the prowl," Flukey lied, trying to sound convincing.

"That shit there... niggaz not going to sleep right until something gives. It's just hard to see a motherfucker getting close enough to clip a nigga like him," Clee said.

"I need you to look into something for me," Flukey said, changing the subject.

"What's that?"

"I need a line on King Von."

"I'll see what I can do, but you know he don't like talking over the phone. And with what just happened to P, he definitely going to be cautious of who he talk to. But let me see what's up."

"That's cool. Just get back at me."

Flukey ended the call and thought about all the shit that was going on. He kind of felt guilty for having a part in Paul getting hit. The more he thought about it, the more shit just didn't add up. Everybody knew Crazy was a grimy-ass nigga, but did he have it in him to fabricate a lie and use King Von's name in vain to get Paul killed? That was the thought cycling around in Flukey's head, and it kind of made sense.

There was a knock at the door. Flukey went to see who it was. He looked through the peephole and saw Rhonda impatiently standing there with one hand on her hip. In the hood they called her Burnt Face. When she was younger she had gotten caught in a house fire and suffered third degree burns over half her body, but you could still see her beauty from before then. She was like one of the guys though.

All Rhonda did was hustle and fuck with the guys. Most of the younger BD's didn't understand how the older guys could rock with her, being that she was from down the hill and the majority of her people were GD's, but Rhonda just fucked with who she fucked with. Both sides respected her because she didn't allow neither faction to put her in the middle of their feuds.

"What's good, Rhonda?" Flukey asked as he opened the door for her.

"Shit. You know why I'm here," she replied, and took the blunt from his hand.

Flukey tossed a bag of powder on the table.

"What the fuck I'm supposed to do with that? I don't know how to cook."

"You gotta come back later then. I'm on something right now."

"Flukey, I need some work. I'm out of everything. I'm broke and I need to hustle," she complained.

"Take this for now and I'll get you together later when I'm done doing what I'm doing." He gave her a plastic zip lock bag full of crack rocks already cut up.

"You heard about Smoke and Gwen getting killed? Mu'fuckas been dropping like flies," Rhonda explained.

"Yeah, Clee was just telling me."

"Fuck Clee bitch-ass," she joked halfheartedly.

Flukey had caught wind of Juvy changing the nigga's life form, but that wasn't something he was going to tell her. They never talked about murders with outsiders.

"Well, I got to go. My car running outside. Make sure yo' lil dirty ass get up with me later."

"I got'chu Rhonda. I just need to go and take care of something." While Flukey was talking, Crazy called.

Rhonda opened the door and walked out as he answered.

"Yo... Aiight... Send me the location, B... Let me get up with Juvy and we'll get on top of it."

Flukey ended the call and grabbed his car keys. He only had one thing to do now – find Juvy.

Be careful of those who look to level the playing field by being deceitful. They hide behind crooked motives. Ones that normally shelter a tyrant...

$$$$$

FLUKEY AND JUVY

Flukey pulled up and picked Juvy up from one of the traps. There was a lot going on and with Paul being taken out of the picture. A power shift was soon to come, and the next up would be Flukey.

Crazy felt as if he should rightfully head the table, but it didn't work that way. However, being that he came home from the joint with word from King Von himself, it made him valid.

"You're not strapped, are you?" Flukey asked Juvy once he got inside the car.

"Yeah,"

"Go tuck it, you won't need it for where we're going."

Juvy went and stashed the gun and got back inside the car. Flukey drove off and headed straight for the express way. Juvy always observed things around him, it was what he did. This game was dangerous, and he used everything to keep himself sharp and ahead of the curve. He was always aware. Flukey taught him that. It took them about an hour and a half to get to where they were going. Juvy never asked any questions, so he had no idea what this was about. He didn't question Flukey, because he trusted him with his own life. Flukey took him in off the streets and showed him nothing but love, and for that alone, Juvy vowed to give him nothing but loyalty and devotion. Flukey pulled up to an apartment building and parked.

"Who live here?" Juvy wanted to know.

"This girl named Keana. I need you to get familiar with her and keep her close. Once you find a way to bump into her, I'll let you know what to do next," Flukey instructed.

"Fuck I'm supposed to do that?"

"You'll figure it out. This has to be done. King Von put emphasis on this being made a priority."

"I'll get it done," Juvy assured him.

"Juvy, don't get caught up in this bitch. She's only a means to an end," Flukey explained.

"I got'chu." Juvy replied. They sat there for a while and waited.

Anytime word came from the joints on behalf of King Von, you knew it had to be something serious. Flukey had no idea what the girl looked like. He was just given an address. They sat out there for nearly 4 hours, and that's when she pulled into the parking lot and headed towards her apartment.

"That's her!" Flukey said, and Juvy looked with intentions to lock her into the folds of his memory. Apparently, she had to be some kind of nurse, because she had scubs on, but that wasn't what caught Juvy's attention. He was drawn in by her beauty. She was extremely beautiful. This was why Flukey said don't get caught up in her – at least that's what Juvy thought.

"Once I get next to her, what then?"

"Honestly, I don't even know, folks. This shit being dictated from the joint. King Von calling the shots on this one personally."

"I'll get it done. I just have to figure out how to approach her without shit seeming weird," Juvy replied and watched as she disappeared in the apartment.

CHAPTER 4
JUVY

Niggaz are always trying to one-up each other, and that's by any means necessary. The thing about growing up in an urban society is that you see a lot of grimy shit, and people using each other for any- and everything. When you're not given any real resources, and are forced to survive with what little you do have, your environment becomes a dog-eat-dog world. It's a dangerous game nonetheless, but it's the nature of the business.

The block was always live and eventful. There were days filled with chaos, but that wasn't always the case. The thing about the hood was that you never knew what kind of day it would be. For the most part, there was more drama than good times. So, when everything was going well and people were having a ball, those were the days you counted as blessings.

Juvy was sitting on the porch with Zo.

Zo was one of the guys, just from another faction of Disciples. He was one of those guys that came around every now and then. He chased the money and was known for being a solid, stand-up nigga. Zo was probably one of the few who wasn't BD, but got treated as if he was, and he had a free pass through the hood. It was common to have niggaz like that. Zo was thorough, and Juvy took an extreme liking to the nigga. He appreciated real niggaz, and knew what Zo brought to the table intellectually. Juvy saw him as someone worth having a conversation with.

"I want to ask you something, just between the two of us," Juvy told him.

"Shoot."

"I met this dude, and we got to taking about God and shit. It caught my attention. I never gave any of my time to God before, and it just had me thinking about a lot of shit. Do you believe in God?"

"That's a sticky topic, but I know where you're coming from. Honestly, I've always had belief in God, and felt connected to my faith, but we all have our shortcomings. Why are you really asking these questions?" Zo wanted to know.

There was a brief moment where Juvy was quiet. He wanted to choose his words carefully.

"I'm still trying to figure that part out. I'on't plan on being a street nigga for the rest of my life. We're out here taking chances everyday, and we slide by without mention. Fuck that! I feel like I have a purpose. I just need to find out what it is."

"I mean, you make a valid point, but you need to understand one thing. A nigga with a conscience can be dangerous to himself. When you're in the jungle with other predators, you can't afford to think in terms of decency. But at the same time, this game will kill you. Not so much literally, but on the physical plane. And in knowing that, you have to balance what you have to be with what you need to be. That's the reality of the streets. Just hold on to who you are on the inside and try not to lose sight of that. But in the end, we always lose some part of who we are. You sound like you still have a bit of good left inside you though, and if that's true, do yourself a favor and hold on to it," Zo explained.

Juvy couldn't find any words to express how he felt in that moment, so he just remained quiet.

"Don't let this game destroy you lil' homie. When you decide to save face in these streets, be sure to save yourself as well."

Juvy couldn't find any words to express what he was feeling on the inside, he just knew something was there. The guilt was there as well. Guilt from all the things he'd done, as well as the things he knew he still had to do.

The street lights were starting to come on. The sky went from friendly blue to timid grey, but people were still enjoying themselves; dancing and playing around in the streets. Juvy sat back and smiled as he watched two little girls jumping rope. This was only a glimpse of the other side. The side of good fortune in the hood. And although it was often short lived, he had to take whatever peace he could find. But of course, it was all too good to be true.

As if the smiles, laughter, and abundance of positive energy had been brewing for far too long, a relentless wrath of rage stormed through. All of a sudden, gunfire broke out and people started scattering about. Pandemonium had struck like bolts of lightning, fucking everything up.

Bladadah!

Bladadah!

Bladadah!

Bladadah!

A slew of machine guns went off simultaneously. It sounded like the shooters were in competition with each other to empty as many clips as possible. Juvy was caught in a trance – staring as the gunmen fired from separate gangways. Then, he remembered the little girls who were jumping rope only a few feet away from the shooters. He jumped off the porch and ran full speed around a van, not really caring if he got hit. He was willing to give his life for theirs. He realized he didn't even have a gun, but it still didn't matter.

By the time he made it to the other side of the van, it was too late. Their small lifeless bodies were nestled together in a fetal position, soaked in their own blood and riddled with bullets. Juvy fell to his knees and looked on in utter shock as he heard what must have been a mother's shriek in the distance. Disbelief carried his emotions to a cold and bitter place. A place he knew all too well. These were the very acts that made him question God. I mean, how could there be a God? How could he let their lives be taken so soon? Tears fell from his face and it felt like his heart had been shattered. This was why he chose not to believe; because God never gave him any reason to.

I followed you into the pits of hell and fought the flames that threatened the city, only asking God for a sign that my faith wouldn't be consumed in vain. Instead, I was left underneath the rubble and debris of my own pity, asking God why He had forsaken me and left me alone in a battle being fought in His name...

$$$$$

YATTA

Stateville Correctional Center

Yatta was from the Buff. After he got locked up for a murder, a lot had changed for the worst in the hood, and others rose in power. That was common when niggaz got locked up. Buff City had flipped and there was a new culture brewing. He had been locked up for quite some time, but that didn't keep him out of the loop. The news about Paul had hit him hard and he knew it was foul play. Although he and Crazy were both from the same hood, they were polar opposites and didn't really see eye to eye. Yatta never allowed his personal feelings to alter the business – Nation business, that is. Crazy was once their appointed Chief, but had lost his authority when he went to prison. The same had happened to Yatta. Like I said before, when one Chief falls, another rises in power.

Clee had gotten word inside for Yatta to call him. Yatta figured it was to get a message to King Von, because he never directly dealt with issues on the streets unless he absolutely had to.

Yatta made sure the coast was clear before slipping into the janitor's closet. He removed a small cellphone from a hole in the moldy drywall and made the call.

"What's the word?"

"Flukey trying to holla at Von. I didn't want to reach out to him without you knowing," Clee explained.

"Why?" Yatta was curious.

"I really don't know, but if he's asking, I'm sure it's something important."

"I'll pass the word. What's being said about that move against P?" Yatta wanted to know.

"Mu'fucka's really don't know. The streets ain't really saying shit," Clee exposed. "It's some sneaky shit going on behind that," he added.

"I got my suspicions too, but I need to dig a lil' deeper before I speak on shit. What's to the nigga Crazy – how he been acting?"

"I'ont really know. I try to keep clear of him. Why, wassup?"

"Just asking," Yatta lied. He didn't want to expose certain things to anyone until he got all the facts straight.

"I got to slide, but you'll hear from me soon," Yatta said, then ended the call.

$$$$$

As it turned out, the two little girls that were killed were visiting from out of town. It was their first time in Chicago, and just like that, they had become a part of the vicious cycle that claimed the lives of so many innocent people plagued by the gun violence in the city. The powers that be can pretty much tolerate us killing each other, but when someone kills a kid, all bets are off and someone has to answer for it.

Juvy was in a dark place, and there was really no way to pull him out of it. He knew who was responsible for the shooting, and he wouldn't rest until they paid for it. The police had the hood on lock. They patrolled the streets with authority. Nobody was making any money, and niggaz were getting locked up for anything from jaywalking, to spitting on the sidewalks. This affected everybody, and when there was no money being made, shid, everything else was just pointless.

Juvy was crouched inside the trunk of a stolen Buick, and his mind was in a fit of rage. He didn't care if he lived or died. His heart was colder than a frigid December's eve. Flukey had never seen that side of him, and it even scared him. He had tried talking Juvy away from the edge, but it was all in vain. It wasn't about respect for Juvy. For him, it was more about doing the right thing. Juvy didn't care about anything or anyone. He was a loner, and lost within the pastures of his own internal conflict. Life wasn't really worth anything to him, and he knew these kind of thoughts weren't ideal or conducive to his well-being, but it was what it was.

The car slowed down. Juvy clenched the Mosburg shotgun and readied himself for what was to come. This mission was personal, so he had recruited two of his most trusted friends to accompany him. Chris, who was also Flukey's older brother, was driving the stolen car, and another BD named Romy, who went to school with Juvy growing up, sat in the passenger seat.

As he drove into their rival's territory, Chris noticed a bunch of people sitting on top of cars in a parking lot. He turned into an alley and came up around 118th and Indiana. Chris killed the lights on the Buick and backed into the other side of the lot. It didn't appear to be suspect, because the people who lived in the back houses normally backed their cars into the parking lot for an easier drive out. Once he felt like he was close enough, Chris popped the trunk and Juvy went to work.

BOOM!

BOOM!

The buckshots from the shotgun scattered as people started fleeing the scene. Juvy aimed and hit whoever was in range. Romy was standing beside him shooting as well.

BOC!

BOC!

BOC!

BOC!

BOC!

Romy hit one of the guys fleeing. Juvy hopped the gate and stood over him.

BOOM!

He blew his brains out against the concrete, then ran around the front and continued shooting until he ran out of ammunition. There was a bat leaning against one of the houses and he went for it. Juvy chased someone down and clipped them from behind. The man did an awkward front flip and crashed into the side of the car.

Juvy brought the bat down on his head with a sickening thud, and continued to hit him profusely. Chris pulled up.

"Juvy, let's go!" he yelled, but his plea was ignored. Juvy was beating the guy so badly that he nearly decapitated him.

"Go get him," Chris told Romy.

"We got to go, bro!" Romy said in an attempt to get Juvy off the guy, but he wasn't hearing it.

BOOM!

BOOM!

BOOM!

A barrage of gunfire went off as men came running out of the gangway. Juvy took one last swing, then took off running towards the awaiting car. When he made it to the car, he was struck by a round as he dove into the back seat. Chris pulled off in a haste, then noticed there was blood splattered everywhere inside the car.

"Juvy hit!" Romy yelled, and told him to hang on.

He had caught a bullet in his side.

"I think it went straight through," Juvy said, as he winced in pain, then put pressure on the wound with his hands.

They couldn't go to a hospital because they would have to call the police and report a gunshot victim, but he was losing a lot of blood and in desperate need of a doctor.

"He's fading back here," Romy said, as he smacked Juvy's face keeping him awake. "Don't go to sleep, bro," Romy added, and tried his best not to panic. Chris had no idea what to do. He called his brother Flukey, and told him what happened. After listening carefully to Flukey's instructions, Chris sped towards the expressway.

$$$$$

Juvy finally came around and noticed he was in a hospital bed and gown. He sat up and felt a sharp pain in his side. As he gathered himself, a nurse walked in.

"You're finally up," she said, and began checking his vital signs.

"Where am I?"

"You're in Mount Rush Hospital. Can you tell me what you remember?"

"Not much."

"Well, you were dropped off by a good Samaritan. Apparently, you were a victim of a drive-by shooting. They got you here just in time though. A moment later, and you would've bled to death," the nurse explained, then left the room before he could ask any more questions.

Juvy managed to get out of the bed and stand on his feet. He'd passed out in the back of the Buick, and that's pretty much all he remembered. The walk to the waiting room area was agonizing and painful. He needed to find a phone. The one in his room didn't dial out. He wasn't having much luck finding one, but that didn't stop him from searching around some more. After enduring a few more minutes of tiresome steps, he leaned against a wall. His legs were weak and he didn't have much energy.

"You don't look too good. Are you alright?" he heard a voice ask from behind. When he turned to see who it was, he was taken aback. It was her... the girl from the house that Flukey had drove him to. Her name was Keana.

"I'm good. You a nurse?"

"Well, not technically – yet. I'm doing my intern hours and I graduate from med-school soon."

"I know this might sound kind of crazy, but I have no idea where I am."

"You're – in a hospital," Keana replied, a bit skeptical of his statement.

"I can see that," Juvy replied, and looked down at his gown and footies.

"I'm talking about where?"

"You're in Chicago Heights."

"Of course I am."

"I think you should probably get some more rest. You need it," Keana suggested.

"I think I've slept long enough. How long until I can leave this place?"

"That's not a call I can make. It's up to the doctor."

"Fuck that, I'm out."

"You think that's a good idea?"

"I'm not used to making good decisions. Look how far that's gotten me," Juvy said sarcastically.

"I'm not sure if you meant that as a compliment, but if you did, you should come up with something else," Keana laughed.

Juvy was extremely attracted to her, and that's when it hit him. He was brought to this hospital for a reason. Him getting shot was an opportunity for an introduction. An introduction to her. It was like killing two birds with a single stone. He still had no idea exactly what she had to do with anything, or who she was connected to, but he hoped to find out.

It was awfully tragic how innocent people were placed in the cross hairs of other's misdeeds, and often made victims of unfortunate circumstances.

"You think you can give me a ride back to the city?"

"I'm afraid not. I'd lose everything I've been working so hard for if I did. It's unethical."

"I can respect that. What if I wanted to get to know you outside of this place?"

"I'm not sure that's possible. Besides, I don't deal with guys from the streets."

"And how do you know where I'm from?"

"Let's not play that game, because you know I'm right. I'm just not into losing people to that side of the tracks anymore."

"Life isn't that simple, but I get it. At least you know what you want out of life. I'm still figuring my shit out. I guess being honest about it is a start," he admitted, then took a seat on the bench.

"It's not too late for you. You just have to give yourself a fighting chance," explained Keana.

"You sound like you're trying to lecture me, but I understand your point of view – I really do."

"I'm not trying to come off that way, I just hate seeing so many of our Black men go to prison and get shot dead in the streets."

"That's the story of my life," Juvy said, and stood to his feet.

His bandages were bleeding.

"We need to change those."

Keana took him back to his room and retrieved some fresh gauzes and medical tape. After cleaning his wound, she put some ointment and new bandages on him.

"You're pretty good at that," Juvy complemented.

"I like helping people."

"So why not help me?"

"Because you have to help yourself first."

"Lead the way and I'll follow."

"You're just not letting up. Okay, next week I'll be volunteering at the food pantry in Riverdale, helping feed the homeless. You can meet me there."

"I guess I'll see you then," Juvy replied.

Keana smiled and left the room.

The day was dragging by and Juvy really wanted to get up and leave, but he figured he would use this time to get his mind right. Seeing those little girls' lifeless bodies riddled with bullets had done something to him mentally. He was trying to give the whole God thing a go, but shit like that was making it extremely hard to believe. When he was bleeding out in the back of the Buick, there wasn't an ounce of fear in his heart. I wouldn't go as far as to say that he was suicidal, but he damn sure wasn't far from it neither.

Lord please protect me from my friends, because I can handle my enemies…

CHAPTER 5
CRAZY

The game was cold, and for the most part, Crazy accepted all that came with it. This was the world he had belonged to for longer than he could remember.

Back in 2007 he was pulled over by the blue and whites and it wasn't a typical traffic stop. Nawl, I'm talking about guns drawn, bull horns, and all the other accessories required on a high-alert traffic detail. Crazy knew something was up, he just didn't know what. At the time he'd recently been released from prison, so he wasn't out long enough to be in trouble. Plus, his driver's license was valid. *What the fuck is this about?* That thought ran rapidly through his head.

After pulling over and following all the instructions given to him, Crazy was removed from his car. It was a familiar routine for him. Not a comfortable one, but definitely familiar. As he sat in the back seat of the police car, he noticed another unmarked car pull up. A detective got out and approached the vehicle he was in. He told Crazy that he was investigating a murder. Crazy shrugged it off and told him he was just recently released from prison, but as it turned out, the investigation was for a cold-case murder.

The ride to the police station was both agonizing and perplexing. Crazy was raking his brain to remember any murders he knew about, and there were still blanks. He had done so much in the streets, that it was hard to keep track of the bodies.

Eventually he was charged, tried and convicted for the shooting death of a man he'd never met a day in his life. The most confusing part of it all was the evidence used against him at trial. The prosecutor produced a concealed tracking device on his car that placed him at the crime scene, and somehow there were also wiretaps. All of those things threw him for a loop, and it was in that instance that he knew he had been set up!

As Crazy drove down the street reminiscing, he saw Juvy get on a bus. He just wasn't sure of him. At least not as convinced as Flukey was about the lil' nigga. After being set up for the cold-case murder, Crazy had vowed to never allow anyone else determine his fate, and killing Paul had made Juvy a liability – one that Crazy didn't want falling into his lap. He pulled out his phone and called Juvy.

"Yo?" Juvy answered.

"What's to it, B, where you at?"

"I'm at the trap," Juvy lied. "Why, wassup?"

"Just checking in on you. You know, making sure you're good."

"I'm straight."

"Who all there with you right now?"

"I'm in the basement right now."

"I'll let you get back to it then. I think one of these days we should circle a block and chop it up."

"Yeah, one of these days," Juvy replied, ending the call.

"Lying-ass nigga!" Crazy spoke out loud to himself.

He continued following the bus for quite a distance, and when Juvy finally got off, he walked across the street into a church.

"Fuck this nigga doing?" Crazy was confused.

Moments later, a Dick Boy (unmarked-car detective) pulled up and headed into the same church. That really caught Crazy's attention, and to make matters worse, it was a detective he knew. His name was Officer Jones. He used to work the streets in the neighborhood as a beat cop, but had made detective some years later. *What's the odds of this*? He wondered.

"I knew that lil' nigga couldn't be trusted," Crazy said as he pulled his phone out and made a call.

"Yeah?"

"Ya boy foul."

"Fuck you talkin' 'bout?"

"Juvy! The nigga ain't right."

"Man, you still on that shit? Shorty good. I don't never have to worry about him." Flukey was sure of it.

"Okay, let me tell you what I know. So, I'm sitting at a red light and see the lil' nigga get on the bus. Something told me to follow him, so I did just that. While doing so, I called 'em and asked where he was at. He lied and said he was in the trap. Right then my radar went up. I continued following him and ended up near Calumet City some-damn-where. Then, he gets off the bus and walks into a church –"

"The lil' nigga probably found God," Flukey interjected sarcastically.

"I guess Detective Jones did too then, because he went into the same church a short while later."

"What'chu suggesting?"

"I'm saying we need to look closer at what he's doing."

"Let me hit'chu back. I'ma call him."

"Don't say shit about what I just told you."

"I got this," Flukey assured him.

Crazy tossed his phone onto the passenger seat and continued to watch the church. He had no idea what Juvy was up to, but he was going to get to the bottom of it.

$$\$\$\$\$\$$

JUVY

He had to get away from the hood and let his mind relax. He felt like he couldn't breathe at times. Especially being around the hood and all the problems that came with it. For some odd reason, the bus seemed peaceful. He could ride through the city and peer out of the windows, watching as people went about their daily lives without a care in the world. He didn't have to worry too much, or look over his shoulder every other second. He could fall asleep and nothing bad would ever happen to him. He knew one of these days he was going to get killed, though. He just didn't want to die today. Maybe not tomorrow or the next day, neither.

Juvy was having a hard time adjusting to where his life was heading, opposed to where he wanted it to be. There was a lot going on around him, and it was really starting to take a toll on him. While Juvy was in his head, his phone rang. He didn't bother looking at the caller ID, which he regretted the moment he heard Crazy's voice. Crazy had been trying to get personal with him and build a relationship, but Juvy just wasn't into it. He would always leave the room or get out of the car whenever he would come around. It wasn't nothing personal, Juvy just didn't like his vibe and chose to disregard any of the company he offered.

"Yo," Juvy answered.

"What's to it, B, where you at?"

"I'm at the trap. Why, wassup?" Juvy lied.

"Just checking in on you. You know, making sure you're good."

"I'm straight."

"Who all there with you right now?"

For some reason, it felt like a trick question and Juvy knew he shouldn't have answered it, but before he could stop himself, his lips were already in motion.

"I'm in the basement right now," Juvy lied.

He knew he had fucked up in some way, but he didn't have to answer to Crazy. Fuck 'em!

"I'll let you get back to it. I think one of these days we should circle a block and chop it up."

"Yeah, one of these days." Juvy hung up and got off the bus.

As he climbed the stairs to the church, he thought about Keana for some reason. She had a good spirit and good energy about her. Although he didn't know her, she just seemed like the right person to fit into his life, but he had no idea how she was tied into the reasoning of Flukey wanting him to get next to her.

What if he was ordered to kill her – could be do it? Juvy asked himself those questions constantly. He wanted to follow the path of self-awareness he was on and figure out who he was on the inside. It wasn't so much about finding God, it was more about him finding himself.

"I'm glad you could make it out. I want you to meet a friend of mine," Brother James said the minute Juvy walked into the church.

"A friend?" Juvy was confused.

"He's a good dude. His name is Detective Jones–"

"Yo, I'm not into kicking it with twelve – I'll pass on that," Juvy cut him off.

"It's nothing like that. He's actually from your neighborhood. I told him about you and he's excited to meet you. He runs a program for –"

"I think you lost me with this one. I'm not interested. I only decided to deal with you because I wanted to learn more about God. That's it!"

As Juvy was talking, a tall guy in a suit walked in. He approached the two of them and greeted Brother James.

"Detective Jones. I was just telling Juvy about you, and he voiced that he's uncomfortable with this ordeal." Brother James was straight forward.

"I can understand that, but let me say this... I know right now a lot of things don't make sense, but God has a plan for you. When I first met Brother James, I was arresting him, so know that we're men that can make mistakes in life and still be here for each other at a later time."

"Detective Jones helped me find God, and I've been a believer ever since," added Brother James.

"That's cool and all, but like I said, I can't deal with twelve."

"Just take my card, and if you ever feel the need to talk, hit me up."

Juvy took the card from the detective and slipped it into his pocket, then turned and walked out the door.

Juvy sat on the bench waiting for the bus. He couldn't believe Brother James had tried him like that. He was pissed. His phone started ringing. It was Flukey.

"What's up, bro?"

"Where you at?" Flukey wanted to know.

"I'm waiting on the bus."

"Fuck you doing at a bus stop – where you at?"

"Real shit... I been talking to this dude and shit... the nigga like a preacher or some shit. I've been trying to find some answers, so I be stopping by his church and shit," replied Juvy.

Flukey smiled on the inside because he knew Crazy was wrong. Juvy was thorough.

"I'm about to come grab you. We can stop at a store or something and get'chu some holy water and a bible, nigga," Flukey joked.

"Fuck you, nigga!"

"Sit tight, I'm on my way."

Life hides its secrets. Burys them so no one will ever be able to find them. But be aware; like most treasures, they hardly ever go undiscovered...

$$$$$

Stateville Correctional Center

Juvy had no idea why he elected to travel up to the prison to meet a complete stranger. Although Yatta was from Buff City, that wasn't enough to make it a comfortable trip. They had never met because prison kept Yatta off the streets. At first, Juvy wasn't going to go, but he decided he had nothing to lose by doing so. He was curious about their conversation, and wondered what else he could learn about Yatta that he hadn't already heard. Shit was crazy, and Juvy knew that the more he indulged in the chaos, the harder it would be to separate himself from it all.

After going through the searches and clearing the other security measures to get inside the prison, Juvy felt violated and disrespected. This was his first time inside an institution and it would definitely be his last. He was escorted to the visiting room and directed to a four-sided metal table. As he sat there waiting for Yatta, he realized he had no idea what he looked like. After a short while, a big dude with long dreads came walking down the stairs. Juvy could sense it was him, and from the look of it, Yatta was familiar with what he looked like too, because he headed straight for Juvy's table.

"I see you finally made your way up here," Yatta said, and sat down.

The nigga looked like the rapper Ace Hood, and had a dominating personality that separated him from a lot of niggaz Juvy had ran across in the streets.

"I'm here. So, what do you know about my father?"

"Yo' pops was a real nigga, but he fell victim to some fucked up circumstances," Yatta began to explain.

"You're steady saying 'was', like in the past tense. You got the wrong nigga. My pops isn't dead. The nigga just a deadbeat, and I don't fuck with him on no bases," Juvy snapped.

"Listen, I don't know who been feeding you the lies that got you all screwed up, but your pops just got killed recently."

"You really got the wrong dude."

"Nawl, I don't. It's a lot of shit you don't know, and I can fill those voids for you if you want me to, but the shit is deep. It's not really my place to send you down that road unless you're ready to go."

"I think you've wasted both of our time because my pops is somewhere fucking someone else's life up. He's not dead!"

"Yo, you're so far off track, it's not even funny."

"The fuck you know about me? You don't know shit!"

"I know more than you think I know. Like, yo' O.G. only started getting high once King Von got locked up. P tried to save her, but she was already too far gone," Yatta said as Juvy rose to his feet.

"Man, you'on't know what the fuck you talking about. My O.G. ain't got shit to do with King Von... and P? Yeah, you got jokes," Juvy snapped, and was told to remain sitting or the visit would be terminated.

"You think you ended up where you are as a coincidence? King Von took the ride for his brother on a murder rap they committed back in the day. He took the ride and made Paul promise to uphold certain obligations. P took control of the streets and Von placed orders from here – in this same prison you're in right now. Paul was told to make sure your O.G. was taken care of, which he did. She started getting high, and P fed her addiction to keep her from running the streets. He never intended for things to get out of control. They fell in love with each other and tried their best to hide it from King Von, but he found out. The feud they had wasn't about power or money. It was over Georgette-Goldy. Your O.G."

Juvy was trying to process everything Yatta had just said and find a clear head space to come up with a reasonable explanation for the accusations, but his mind was drawing blanks.

"So, you're telling me that King Von is my father?" Juvy inquired.

"Not at all. Paul was your father."

Hearing that made Juvy sick to his stomach, and now a lot of shit was starting to make sense. He vividly remembered the intense gaze in P's eyes and the familiarity of energy that made him feel connected to him.

"How?"

"They were dealing with each other behind King Von's back and never got caught," Yatta added.

"So, why has this other nigga been claiming to be my pops?"

"Phil was just a nigga your O.G. dealt with from time to time when she and Paul separated. It was the story she told, and it was the story we ran with."

"So, how do you know this story about P being my father is true?"

"Because I was the one that helped them sneak behind King Von's back. When your mother got pregnant, she asked me not to tell Von, then she broke up with Paul and started a relationship with Phil to cover up the pregnancy."

"I got to go – I need some air," Juvy said.

"Yo, don't let them niggaz out there use you to fight their battles."

"I think it's too late for that."

With that, Juvy left the visiting room and went to find some kind of resolve.

CHAPTER 6
FLUKEY

Flukey hadn't been to the trap in a couple of days and figured it was time to make an appearance. Niggaz in the hood were on high alert, but that was the norm. The bodies that fell on their rival's side weren't going to go without retaliation. Twelve had the streets on fire, but that only lasted for so long. Flukey was stressed the fuck out with all the shit that was going on. Plus, Crazy was driving on him reckless about Juvy not being a trustworthy nigga. Shit was just all over the place.

Flukey walked into Juvy's room. Juvy was gone. Flukey wanted to see how things were going with Keana. He didn't mind putting in work for the Mob, he just hated flying blind. He had no idea what the chick had to do with anything. Flukey was just told to keep an eye on the bitch. Those orders came from King Von. He had been granted a new trial and she was somehow being used as a pawn.

Flukey looked around for nothing in particular, then sat down on the bed. Juvy had been moving around a lot lately, but it wasn't anything out of the sorts. Juvy was like that – a loner. But whenever Flukey called, he would come running, and that's all he could ask for.

Juvy had clothes all over the room. Flukey decided to put some of his things away. After grabbing a trash bag for the dirty clothes, he went to work. He always checked the pants and hoodie pockets before sending them to get washed, because one time he had accidently washed $600 of Juvy's money. Lesson learned. Flukey went through everything and made sure not to make that same mistake again. He made it to the last pair of pants, and as he went through the pockets, he found a small business card. Flukey's face went from a curious gaze to a stale expression. It was a card that read; DETECTIVE LAWRENCE JONES. Flukey stood to his feet and balled his fists in disbelief. Crazy was right. Juvy was meeting with a detective that day at the church. But why? Fuck that – there could only be one explanation for talking to a homicide detective.

"Fuck!" Flukey yelled, then pulled his phone out and did the one thing he was reluctant to do. He called Crazy.

$$\$\$\$\$\$$$

JUVY

Juvy walked into the food pantry and looked around for Keana. It didn't take long to find her, and she was all smiles. She had a good personality to match her looks. She was fine, and Juvy wanted to get to know her better. Keana had to be no older than 30 years old, and was completely different from what he was accustomed to. Juvy had never done anything remotely close to feeding the homeless before. He was used to them begging for change or alcohol. Keana walked from around the serving counter to greet him. She even looked more beautiful than before.

"I thought you weren't going to show up. Guess I was wrong," she said.

"Judging me wrong already. But that's cool, I don't mind proving people wrong," he joked back.

"Well, we have to get started before the lines come pouring in. Here, you'll need to put this on," she handed him a hair net and an apron.

Juvy felt so out of place and silly that he couldn't help but stick out like a sore thumb.

"Relax. You don't have to impress anyone here," Keana said. She could sense he was nervous.

"I'll try."

"That's all we can do."

Keana escorted him behind the counter and gave him a scooper to place food items on the trays as the homeless came through the line. When the doors opened, people flooded the pantry. The air went from a fresh to a stale odor. The lines were extremely long, and it seemed as if they would never end.

"So, where are you from?" she asked Juvy, making small talk while they served the patrons.

"I'm from the southside of Chicago."

"I'm from the southside as well."

"Seriously?"

"Yup, born and raised."

"Where 'bout?" Juvy was curious. He'd been on the southside his entire life. There was no way possible a girl as fine as her would have slipped past him.

"I'm from the Roseland area," she replied.

Juvy instantly turned his face up. The Buff was basically Roseland.

"I'm from Buff City. How is it that we've never bumped heads?"

"You're from over there?" she inquired, surprised.

"Why you say it like that?"

"I'm from the other side of the tracks – you know how that goes. My father got killed when I was younger. He and my people would go back and forth with the BD's from Buff City – which I'm assuming you're one of right – a BD?"

"Yeah, but I'm trying to walk away from that life-style. Back to your people... who was your father?"

"I really shouldn't be talking about this."

"I'm not looking for any problems, nor am I trying to bring any your way. I just want to know," Juvy assured her.

"My father's name was J-Prince."

Juvy was young when he got killed, but he knew exactly who he was. Everybody knew J-Prince. He was the biggest name from across the tracks back in his day. More importantly, it wasn't so much about who he was, it was about who had killed him. King Von was doing time for the death of her father. Juvy's silence made her uncomfortable.

"You knew my father, didn't you – or at least you heard of him?"

"I'm not really sure," Juvy lied.

"Well, that life is behind me now. You said you used to be a BD, or are you trying to walk away?"

"I'm trying to walk away. I just don't know how," he admitted.

"I have a cousin who used to be with my father. He was very violent and had a bad reputation back in the day. He did time in prison and found God along the way. Now I'm not super religious or anything like that, but I do believe in God, and that things don't just happen – they happen for a reason. If my cousin can change, you can too. He should be here shortly. I'll introduce the two of you, and if you like, you can pick his brain."

"I appreciate the gesture, but this is a battle I have to figure out on my own for now," Juvy replied.

They continued to serve food and talk about their past. She was cool, and Juvy really took a liking to her. He didn't want to let his ties to the death culture ruin him having a good life, and if walking away from the guys was the route he had to take, then so be it.

Keana asked if he would go into the back and get the pan of corn. Juvy obliged. Feeding the homeless wasn't that bad, he actually enjoyed volunteering. When he made it back up front, he froze dead in his tracks. Brother James was talking to Keana. He hadn't seen him since their last conversation and run-in with Detective Jones. It was a small world. Juvy had no idea why he was here, but then again, a lot of churches helped out with food drives. He slowly approached the two of them, and Brother James' eyes lit up.

"Juvy! What are you doing here?" he asked, surprised.

"Wait, you two know each other?" Keana was perplexed.

"Yeah, he came by the church and we talked a few times. He's seeking himself right now," Brother James replied.

"I was just telling him that I had a cousin who changed his life, and you two already know each other," Keana said.

Juvy was floored by this added revelation. Brother James was her cousin *and* J-Prince was her father? What else was there to know?

"What brings you here? I can see you've met my little cousin."

"Yeah, we met at the hospital after I got shot."

"Shot – when?" Brother James asked, genuinely concerned.

"Not too long ago. Keana, I got to make a run real fast – something came up," Juvy said, and left before she could say anything.

Juvy was walking down the street thinking about all the shit that had been going on. He had no idea where things went wrong, but there was no turning back now. He turned the corner and ran into an instant problem – the GD's from the other side. He turned back around and they got right on his trail.

BOOM!

BOOM!

BOOM!

Bullets were flying past his head and hitting cars and other objects. He didn't have a chance to shoot back because they were relentless in their pursuit. Juvy was only a few blocks away from his hood, but when you had niggaz on your ass trying to fill you up with hot lead, that journey could feel like it was miles away.

Stank and Burger didn't let up, and Juvy knew he would be a prized kill under their belts. Both of them were known shooters for the GD's, and that meant trouble for him. Burger wasn't as fast as Stank, but when you're behind a trigger, you really don't have to be fast at all.

Juvy ducked behind a car and pulled his gun out. Once he caught his breath he looked up.

BOOM!

BOOM!

BOOM!

BOC! BOC! BOC! BOC! BOC!

Burger and Stank sent him running for cover. Juvy shot back as he made his way down an alley. Pausing for a moment to catch his breath again, he pressed his back up against a garage and pulled out his phone. He called Flukey.

"Yo?" Flukey answered.

"These niggaz on my ass. I need you to slide through," Juvy informed him in a panic.

"Where you at?"

"I'm a couple blocks over in the alley near Prairie. Burger and that nigga Stank shooting at me."

"We're on our way," Flukey said, and ended the call.

$$$$$

CRAZY AND FLUKEY

Flukey sat in the front seat while Crazy drove. Although Flukey had some questions for Juvy, that could wait. At the end of the day, he was still family,

151

and one of the guys. Flukey loved Juvy, and if he called, he would come running. "Where the fuck he say he was at?" Crazy asked as he drove with his eyes peeled.

"He should be in the alley right ahead," Flukey replied, just as shots rang out.

"Fuck that – let me out," Flukey said, and jumped out of the car before it could come to a complete stop.

He raced towards the gun shots. If anything bad happened to Juvy, he would never forgive himself. When he made it to the alley, he immediately spotted Burger.

BOOM!

BOOM!

BOOM! BOOM! BOOM!

Flukey shot with all intentions to kill, and sent Burger ducking.

Juvy appeared and ran towards Flukey.

"I'm out!" Juvy yelled.

BOC! BOC! BOC! BOC! BOC! BOC!

BOOM!

BOOM!

BOOM!

Stank and Burger reemerged, and fired multiple rounds nearly killing them both. Flukey shot back as police sirens were heard in the distance.

EEERRRKKK!!!

BOC! BOC! BOC!

Crazy came around the alleyway – tires screeching as he shot from the window. He pulled up next to Juvy and Flukey.

"Let's roll!" he yelled, and they got in the car then fled the scene.

When the trio made it safely to the trap, Flukey gave their guns to one of the guys to stash. Flukey was glad to have Juvy out of harm way, but he needed to have a sit-down with him.

"Crazy, let me holla at Juvy real quick," Flukey said, indicating he wanted some privacy.

"I'll be upstairs," Crazy replied, and he got out the car.

"Yo, what's up with you? Lately you've been acting real weird. I hope it don't have shit to do with that religious shit you been on."

"I'm good, bro. You don't have to worry about me – I'm good. You're starting to act like that nigga Crazy," Juvy shot back.

"Where were you a few days ago when Crazy called you?"

"Fuck you mean? I told you, I went to that church."

"And saw who?"

"I went to holla at the preacher nigga."

Juvy was starting to feel some type of way. It was as if Flukey was questioning him. He had never lied to him, and now he was starting to see another side of Flukey – one he'd never seen before.

"Was that the *only* person you saw that day?" Flukey asked, and Juvy let out a sarcastic chuckle.

"That was it, man – I didn't see nobody else."

"I'ma be straight forward with you, and I need you to be honest with me. Did you meet with a homicide detective?"

"Fuck you!" Juvy spat out, and got out of the car.

He slammed the car door and walked away from the trap. In fact, he walked away from it all. Juvy

153

decided he wanted nothing more to do with the guys. After all, he had given them his loyalty and devotion, and in return this was what he got in the end? He got questioned and lied to? No one had ever told him what Yatta had revealed and what was really going on. Juvy didn't have no one to turn to and for the first time in his young life, he felt betrayed and disrespected.

There's really no loyalty amongst thieves. That's normally the ploy initiated just to buy time to rob you of your riches. Thieves value nothing but vanity and bridges that connects them to wealth.

CHAPTER 7
YATTA AND JUVY

Stateville Correctional Center

Juvy went to see Yatta. He was the only person who seemed to know more about what was going on, and he was willing to be honest about shit. Lately Flukey wasn't himself. For some reason, he thought Juvy couldn't be trusted. Juvy had a lot of respect for him, but things were sticky now – in a bad way. Crazy was influencing him, Juvy was almost sure of it. He sat back and listened as Yatta made sense of a lot of shit.

"I know all this may sound like a bunch of lies, but it's not. The hit on Paul was foul play, and I know it'll come to light sooner than later. We'll find out who killed him, and when we do, you know how that'll go."

Juvy didn't reveal to him that he was the one ordered to follow through with the hit.

"Why didn't he let me know he was my father?" Juvy wanted to know.

"That's a question only he can answer. I mean, King Von could possibly shed some light on it, but I'll have to see if he'll be willing to sit down with you.

"He's a very skeptical kind of dude, and you can't fault him for that. Especially with what's going on.

"That nigga Crazy really got it out for me, and I think he's trying to start some shit between me and the guys. When he came around, shit went sour. The nigga toxic."

"You got to watch him, he's sneaky. Gwen and Paul getting killed wasn't a coincidence. I'm sure he had his hands in it."

"What'chu know about a chick named Keana? I was told to get close to her and keep an eye on her. Flukey put me on her and that's all I know."

"I don't know shit about that. I never even heard the name."

"J-Prince was her father," Juvy explained, and Yatta just shook his head.

"You're being used, lil' homie. King Von got a new trial, and shorty's O.G. was a witness to the shooting back in the day. I think they got you sitting on the girl so that when he go back to trial, they'll have you threaten her to make her change her statement. You're basically assuring that King Von will touch the streets again. If shorty don't recant her statement, they'll have you kill her daughter." Yatta was stern and direct.

Juvy was now stuck between a rock and a hard place. This was worse than he'd thought.

"What if I don't do it?"

"You know how this game is played. There's no way around it."

"What if I told you I know who killed my father?"

"Then, I think you should tell me. I mean, I have my suspicion, but it's only an assumption," Yatta replied, and Juvy took a deep breath.

"When Crazy showed up he was real secretive and only talking to certain people. Being that Flukey is our top guy, Crazy only dealt with him. One day they picked me up and told me what we talked about in the car was only between the three of us. I listened as they gave me instructions. They told me it was an order directly from King Von –"

"Grimy motherfuckers. They had you kill your own father. A lot of this shit is making sense to me now. Paul wouldn't bring any harm to you because you were his son. And he wouldn't let anyone else get close enough to him to get the job done. You know they'll never let you walk away from that. You're a liability. That must be what Crazy blew on King Von about before he got out. He told him something, and whatever it was, it was bad enough for Von to have his own brother killed. Damn, shit fucked up."

The guard came into the room and told everyone the visiting room was now closed. Yatta looked him in the eyes.

"Whatever you do, watch your surroundings and don't trust nobody. Crazy is sneaky and he's dangerous. You can't even trust Flukey anymore. Crazy flipped him already. Get away from that nigga before it's too late."

"What if I can't?"

"Then, them niggaz will kill you and get rid of your body."

$$\$\$\$\$\$$$

CRAZY

157

Crazy pulled into the parking lot and saw him standing by the elevator. He was meeting up with Starskie, a crooked cop. He was one of those guys you could pay to do anything. A real grimy-ass nigga. Starskie was on the BD's payroll from back in the day, so he knew Crazy extremely well. Crazy approached him and handed him a brown paper bag.

"I need this done as soon as possible. I got other shit in the works, but this is a key move that needs to happen first," Crazy said.

Starskie opened the bag and thumbed through the bills.

"I never understood you motherfuckers. But as long as it pays like this, who the fuck am I to question anything? I'll get on top of it," Starskie replied, then got inside his car and pulled out of the parking lot.

Crazy hated having to deal with dirty-ass cops. He was sure Starskie had enough dirt on them to send them all to prison for the rest of their lives. The game was played by all kinds of people. Crazy knew one day Starskie would have to go, but for now he was a pawn in the game.

Crazy pulled up to a red light on State Street, and looked down to check his phone. When he looked back up, he saw two men in hoods.

BOOM! BOOM!

The first shot shattered the passenger window, and Crazy stomped on the gas and floored it. He smashed into a van.

BOOM!
BOOM!
BOOM!
BOOM!

BOOM!

BOOM!

His car stalled. Crazy tried to climb out the driver's side door, but it was jammed. He could hear the bullets hitting the car.

Ting! Ting! Ding!

He found his way out of one of the back doors. The assailants ran around the car and continued to shoot at him. Crazy's gun was on the front floorboard in the car, leaving him defenseless. Out of the corner of his eye, he saw a gangway that led to a main street and ran towards that way. He jumped the first gate he approached. They were hot on his trail. Crazy had no idea who they were, but that didn't matter at the moment – surviving was more important. One of the men stopped and fired multiple shots, hitting him in the arm, but it didn't keep him from getting back up and taking off.

BOOM!

BOOM!

BOOM!

They were really trying to kill him, and Crazy was losing a lot of blood.

Whoever it was, wanted him dead. It was broad daylight and here they were full-steam ahead with hot lead.

Crazy made it out onto Michigan Avenue, and ran towards the corner which was the busiest part of the intersection. Both gunmen emerged and started walking towards him. He was cornered and there was nowhere else to run. Crazy tried to get a look at the men pursuing him, but their faces were concealed. One of them raised his gun, taking aim, but stopped when a police cruiser turned the corner. He quickly put his gun away, then wagged his finger at Crazy, indicating that he was a lucky man.

$$$$$

FLUKEY

"The fuck happened to you?" Flukey asked when he walked into the house and saw Crazy's arm in a sling.

Crazy didn't answer right away. He took a drink from the bottle of Remy instead.

"I was in traffic when two niggaz came out of nowhere and opened fire on me. They nearly got me, but it wasn't good enough – I'm here, ain't I?"

"Who was it? I mean, it could have only been them niggaz from across the way."

"Nawl, this was different. It felt personal."

"What's that supposed to mean?"

"It means I just need to pay more attention and watch what's going on around me. But enough about me... I haven't seen Juvy since that day he had his lil' run-in. What's the situation with him?"

"Juvy's good – the lil' nigga just need some time. He's good," Flukey assured him.

"What about the conversation we had? The Detective Jones conversation, to be more specific."

"I looked into it and he didn't know what the fuck I was talking about."

"So, that's it – just let it go?"

"What'chu insinuating – like, what do you want me do? I feel like you're pressing me to do something," Flukey snapped.

"I went looking for some peroxide in the bathroom, and when I couldn't find any there, I decided to look in the pantry – still no luck. That's when it hit me," Crazy snapped his fingers. "Check the bathroom in the master bedroom. Upon my search, I found this underneath a Lysol can."

Crazy placed Detective Jones' card on the table. Flukey just shook his head in disbelief.

"Now there's definitely an explanation for this being there – I'm just hoping it's a good one." Crazy pulled his gun out and placed it beside the card.

Flukey hated to admit the obvious, but he was left with no other choice. "I tried to deal with it on my own and see what the fuck the lil' nigga got going on. I asked him who he met with in that church other than the preacher, and he said nobody. Then, the other day I went into his room to put some of his clothes away and found the card in a pair of pants."

"I knew that nigga wasn't right. Now we got to figure out what the fuck he done told them," Crazy said, then stood to his feet and approached Flukey. He put his hand on his shoulder. "I never questioned you, and I want you to know that, but Juvy gotta go."

"If I thought for one second he was a snitch, I would have no problem saying 'fuck Juvy, I'ma put a bullet in him myself'."

"Man, that's what it is. You got to wake up and call a spade a spade."

"Let me find him, and we'll just go from there."

"You do that."

$$$$$

JUVY

Juvy wasn't sure how Flukey was feeling about him walking off during their last encounter, but he would just have to understand. He felt disrespected that Flukey would insinuate he was a rat. Juvy had been putting in work for the Mob since he was a kid, and to repay him for his loyalty by trying to question if he talked to a detective really made him feel some kind of way. Juvy felt like it was time to put everything on the table and let Flukey know what he knew. Everything. Paul was right; he would have to brace for another storm and live with killing him. There was no taking back what he'd done, but the real problem was Crazy, and how Flukey was being influenced by him.

Juvy didn't want to run into any of the guys until he spoke with Flukey first. There was no telling what Crazy was spreading about him. He would never turn on the Mob, but of course that narrative could easily be altered.

Juvy snuck into the trap unnoticed and climbed the stairs two at a time. He got to the back door and was about to open it until he overheard two men talking. It was Crazy and Flukey. Juvy decided to listen. He peered through the window and noticed that Crazy had a gun on the table next to the card Detective Jones had given him.

"Fuck!" Juvy mumbled to himself.

This was bad. This was definitely something Crazy could use against him and make it seem like he was a snitch. Juvy continued to listen. It was kind of hard to make out exactly what was being said, but he caught the last words spoken by Flukey. "Fuck Juvy, I'ma put a bullet in him myself."

Juvy felt crushed and betrayed. It felt as if his heart had been ripped from his chest. He crept back down the stairs and ran up the alley. The very man that had brought him into the fold was now the same man out to get him.

Juvy got off the bus and walked down the street to the address Keana had given him. The two of them were extremely close now. They would stay up talking on the phone for hours. Juvy voiced how he wanted a different life and something other than gang culture. Keana wanted to save him and be there for him in any way she could. After he left the food pantry, she kind of felt like there was more to the story. Juvy had been through a lot in his young life, and the road was only getting worse. Life was complicated like that. Intricate in the small details. She wanted to save him, but there was only so much she could do. He would have to save himself first.

"Come in," Keana said as she opened the door for him.

Juvy had a look in his eyes that made her feel sad for him. He looked tired and drained. Juvy walked in and sat on the sofa.

"Are you alright?"

"Yeah, I'm good. I just need some sleep. My head is all over the place," he admitted.

"That's cool. I'm here if you want to talk," Keana offered.

Juvy hung his head low and closed his eyes. She sat down next to him and rubbed his shoulders. There was no need in saying anything.

"Sometimes I wish I could start over and do things differently. I've done too much wrong to turn back from my ways," he spoke.

"There's always a chance. You just have to give yourself the opportunity to make a difference."

"I just found out that everything I thought I knew about myself was a lie. I don't know who I am, or where to find the answers."

Then, be the person you want to be, and don't let what's in your past define your future. It's never too late."

Keana wanted to help him badly, but this was a problem only he could help himself with first.

"I need to handle something, and once that's done – I'm out. I'm out for good."

"Well, you do what you have to do. Just be careful. I can tell you why I feel you shouldn't do anything crazy, but then again, it seems like you already have your mind set. Just take care of yourself, and be careful, like I said."

"I will!"

If I die today, remember me. If not, at least try to think about me sometimes...

CHAPTER 8
YATTA

Flukey and Yatta used to be close, but prison has a way of not only separating you from your will, but from the niggaz you once called brothers as well. However, the business was the business and personal shit came second. Buff City stretched across more than twenty blocks, but when Yatta was a free man, they only had a few. Flukey was a day-one nigga, so he'd witnessed the rise and fall of many from the Buff.

"It's been a long time. What's the word?" Flukey said.

"I know, but our ties don't change. I wish things could be different, but unfortunately the circumstances didn't work out that way. Them streets crazy, homie, and I've been hearing some things. I don't like the chatter," Yatta said on the other end of the phone.

"I really don't know what to say about that, because shit is crazy out here. It's not the same. We're enriched in a different culture now."

"What's the story behind P? I want the real – not the watered-down version."

Flukey got quiet for a second. He knew this would come up, and being that Yatta was one of the men that helped place the foundation in place for what the Buff was today, he couldn't lie to him.

"Man, folks – this shit crazy, and there's really no other way to put it. The nigga Crazy came home with word from King Von and sanctioned it. They personally talked and he said it was a go."

"Who pulled the trigger?"

"Shawty – Juvy."

Flukey heard a slight chuckle from Yatta on the other end.

"Other than Crazy, who else know Juvy hit P?"

"I mean, besides King Von – nobody."

"Keep it under wraps for now. I think the nigga Crazy put something in King Von's ear. I just have to figure out what that was. Make sure Juvy keep quiet as well."

"He'll do that anyway."

Flukey decided not to tell him what was going on with Juvy being a rat. That wasn't a conversation to have at the moment.

"I'm about to share something with you, and this don't leave us."

"Fa'sho!"

"That's P's son."

"Who?"

"Juvy, he's P's son."

"Get the fuck outta here!" Flukey was flabbergasted with perplexity.

"Yeah. P didn't want shawty to know, but that's a story only King Von and Paul can tell. It's not my place to shed any light on it. I know bits and pieces from the past, but nothing in fine detail."

"It's some dirty shit going on. You think Crazy know this?"

"I'm not really sure. You got to watch that nigga," Yatta warned.

"I'm already knowing, gang."

"I gotta slide, but I'll reach out to you later," Yatta said, and ended the call.

Yatta made it back to the cell house and headed straight for King Von's cell. He had to pick his brain and figure out what was going on. King Von was a very shrewd and witty guy. He wasn't stupid, and for the most part, he wasn't one of those guys that could be manipulated.

There was always guys standing outside his cell watching over him. I mean, this is the King we're talking about! Yatta was the Institutional Minister. He ran the prison and put together the I-staff that ran the functions. He also had access to King Von, and never had to go through hoops and road blocks to get to him.

"You're back for another lesson?" King Von joked. He and Yatta would play chess for hours and talk about world and prison politics.

"Set it up," Yatta said, then pulled out a stool and got comfortable.

"Sleepy, give us some privacy," Yatta said, and pulled the curtain over the bars.

"What's today's mathematics?" King Von inquired. He was a 5 Percenter, and often spoke in High Science.

"Knowledge, wisdom – all being born to understanding."

"True indeed," King Von replied, and made the first move.

"I had a dialogue with Flukey. He said that situation was handled."

"As it should."

"I'm not really sure what's up with Crazy. The nigga hasn't checked in yet."

"Give him some time. I'm not trying to dictate how you govern you're functions, but this thing with Crazy has to be dealt with differently."

"I'll do just that now that Juvy got shit with shorty in motion. What's the end game?"

King Von had Yatta and Crazy in communication to deal with Keana. She was the key to getting him out of prison. Back in the day, Keana's mother had testified against King Von for the shooting death of J-Prince. The plan was simple; they would use Keana as a pawn to get her mother to recant her testimony. If not, well, you know how the story goes.

"How you holding up on that thing with P?"

"How do you hold up with the death of a brother?" he asked back.

"I've never lost a brother – at least not one blood related, so I don't know."

"Sacrifices come with this game, and we're obligated to make hard decisions. I do what's necessary to keep this train going."

"The streets talking, and they're saying this shit just seems like an inside hit."

Yatta decided to play along the lines of danger. Of course King Von wasn't one to get personal with, but this was the only way to get some answers.

"The streets are always talking. Check!"

"I agree, but sometimes it be worth paying attention to," Yatta replied, and moved his king out of check.

"Just tell me what you know and stop fishing," King Von shot straight.

"The multitude feels like Crazy went home and turned the streets upside down – internally that is. I mean, who else would want P dead?"

"My brother was a man with many secrets, and he played in the gravel for a long time," King Von shrugged, then continued, "I guess it caught up to him. Check."

"You think Crazy would persuade someone to kill P?"

"Crazy did what was asked of him." King Von came straight out with it. "There's things you don't know, and I really don't have to explain them, but because I respect you, and feel like once my time is up you'll be the next to lead, I give you nothing but the utmost admiration and truth. So, if there's things you wish not to know, then don't ask. You're the one person I choose to have this policy with," King Von explained.

Yatta moved his bishop and allowed what was just said to sink in.

"What did Crazy say to convince you to have P killed?" Yatta went straight for the truth.

"My brother and I were always competitive. It made us both strong and vindictive at the same time. We loved each other, but sometimes that isn't enough. We allowed too much pride to fill the voids that replaced our care for each other. When I decided to take the fall for this case, I did so because he was my brother, and I felt there was no need for both of us to spend the rest of our days in a cell. In return, I only asked for his loyalty. He stood true to that until Georgette changed it. He thought I didn't know the two of them had a thing behind my back, then he came –"

"Juvy?" Yatta interrupted, knowing exactly where the conversation was going.

"My brother decided to keep it on the hush, so he never told anyone about the kid. He even separated himself from Georgette, but that's not why I had him put beneath the earth. Paul crossed a line that should've never been crossed. One that broke me in two."

King Von took a minute, and Yatta could see that he was troubled by it still. He'd never seen this side of him.

"This betrayal can't be told to anyone until I finish correcting what my brother did. That's why Crazy was given the okay to kill him, but that was only part of the play. Crazy was only following orders, and a good foot soldier can never be at fault for being a soldier. To sum it all up, my brother made a play that put me on the throne. He wanted me to rise in power, so he played out of bounds and fouled the next man out."

Yatta put what Von was saying together in his head. He vaguely remembered the story about BJ, a.k.a King Shorty.

BJ was ambushed and killed, but no one was ever able to find out who had killed him. That was the man who took King Von under his wing and taught him the game. BJ had groomed him to become who he was today.

"P was the one responsible for killing BJ," Yatta said.

"He ordered the hit and Crazy pulled the trigger."

"And with BJ being out of the picture, you inherited his spot," Yatta stated. He knew this was a dirty game, but damn! That was foul.

Yatta had enough for one day. He had to get some air. These were the men that he watched and admired growing up. The very men that made him want to become a Black Disciple. On the outside, it appeared to be a band of brothers. A brotherhood with genuine love for each other as deep as the deep blue sea.

"I think I need to sleep this off and regroup. I appreciate the honesty, and know that I'll support you until my dying days," Yatta said as he headed for the doorway.

"What about the rest of our game? We've never left a game unfinished."

"Lady x king side bishop – checkmate!"

It has been brought to my attention that what we do as individuals is a reflection upon this Nation and our King, so if we can't come together as one...then, there's no need to come together at all...

CHAPTER 9
FLUKEY

Flukey made it his business to get through to King Von. There were a lot of questions that he needed answers to, and Von was the man who could give him definite answers. Flukey understood why King Von chose not to deal with things personally, but this was one of those situations that required his direct involvement. Yatta told King Von that Flukey needed to holla at him, and he reluctantly agreed. Of course, this was risky, but Flukey had no other options. It wasn't like he could just go up to the prison and visit him or call him directly. Nawl, this took finesse.

King Von had a burner cell, and only a selected few people had a line on him. Everything was for a reason, and what reason could be better than the safety of the King?

"Flukey, what's up? You really went out of your way to get a hold of me. As of lately, a lot of people have been doing the same," Von said.

"Yeah, B, I did, but it's for good reasons."

"Is everything covered on your end?" King Von wanted to know. He was basically inquiring if the line was secure to talk on.

"I just drove out to the boondocks to find a pay phone. I ain't even know they still made these motherfuckers."

"You got my ear."

"I'm pretty sure you know why I'm calling. I've been dealing with Crazy since he's been out, and I can't lie, the nigga done came home and turned shit upside down. I do my part and see to it that shit gets done, but I just need to know if something is true. It came with your name attached to it. Although it's been verified through the Board, I need to know for myself. Did it come from you?"

"That message was valid. That's all I'm willing to speak on about that."

"The streets not really resting well with it, and someone will have to answer for it."

"We all play this game and make moves that's not really in favor of our conscience, but that's how it goes."

"Gwen too?"

"Gwen had nothing to do with what was sanctioned, and if that's an answer you're looking to get from me, then I can't help you there. Paul was my brother, my mother's son. I know what it means to sacrifice for the greater good of the multitude. I'm sacrificing every day."

"So, I take it you already know about Juvy?"

"Unfortunately, I do. Juvy was shielded from the truth –"

"Wait, what'chu talking about?" Flukey was confused. He was talking about Juvy being the one that hit P, but from the words that were coming from Von's mouth, this conversation was headed elsewhere.

"Looks like I ran into something a bit more sticky," Von admitted, then continued, "We're here now... Juvy's mother and I were together for a very long time, and when I took the ride for this murder, we grew apart. Paul was to look after her, which he did, but in doing so, the two of them got too close. Goldy started using drugs, and P was feeding her addiction. They hid their relationship for a number of years, but I knew. When Goldy got pregnant, she disappeared. P didn't know how I would take it, and I think they came up with a ploy to make it seem as if the child belonged to someone else. But when I first saw Juvy, I knew. I knew from the very first picture that I ever saw – he was my nephew," Von explained, and threw Flukey for a loop. He didn't see it coming, not by a long shot.

"Damn, I'on't even know what to say after hearing that shit," admitted Flukey.

"Oh, it gets deeper, I just chose to live with what I know. I gave you your answer and I hope you stand by whatever comes of this conversation. That's my time."

"I appreciate you keeping it real with me, B."

"As we all should. 16!"

$$$$$

Flukey drove through the Buff and thought about the conversation he had with King Von. Juvy was basically Black Disciple royalty, and he could easily inherit the Mob based off that alone. It's crazy how the tables turn.

Juvy had been a ghost and hard to find. Flukey just couldn't see him being a rat. Not him. Juvy had done so much, and if that was the case – shid, even

Flukey would be in cuffs by now. Juvy knew shit about everybody. The bodies dropped by Premo alone would be cause for an immediate manhunt.

Goldy used to be somebody, but that was in the past. Everybody knew she used to fuck with Von back in the day, but that was like ages ago. But P? Nobody knew about that one. Flukey pulled over and parked. He saw Janice and called her over to his car.

"What's up Flukey, you working?"

Janice had grown up in the area, and in her fifty-plus years, she'd seen it all.

"Go down to the trap and tell them I sent you. You seen Goldy?"

"I think she down the hill somewhere. Why, she owe you some money?"

"Nawl, I just need to holla at her, that's all."

"If I see her, I'll let her know," Janice said, and headed down the hill to the trap to get her free bag.

Flukey pulled off from the curb and drove up the street. He hated the circumstances, especially with Juvy. There was only one solution when it came to dealing with rats, and that was putting them down. This was bad.

When Flukey turned up Perry, he ran into Goldy sitting on a porch. He pulled over and parked.

"Goldy, come here and holla at me."

Goldy used to be a beautiful woman. I mean, you could still see what she used to be, but the years of drug use and being on the streets were taking a toll on her. She came up to the car.

"Hey, what's up, Flukey?"

"Jump in, I need to rotate with you real quick."

"This about my son? Because I ain't seen his lil' ass in a few days."

"Nawl, this about something else."

"I got my friend coming through, can it wait?" Goldy asked.

Flukey pulled out a wad of cash, then peeled off a few bills and gave them to her. Goldy got in the car. This had to be serious.

"I know Juvy is P's son, I just need to know what happened between Paul and Von."

"I don –"

"Goldy, I already know, so please don't feed me no bullshit," Flukey said, cutting her off.

Goldy closed her eyes and took a deep breath.

"I knew one day this would come up. I can't do this right now Flukey."

"It's some shit going on and I need you to fill in the blanks."

"I'm not trying to get caught up in nobody's mess."

"And we can keep it that way. I just need to know what's up with Von and P?"

"Okay – okay... When P got locked up, I tried my best to hold on and do right by him, but when I couldn't find a way to cope, I started using drugs. I lost myself, and I felt so alone. The only person I had to help me was Paul. He didn't approve of me getting high, but he promised that if I stayed off the streets, he would make sure I had drugs. We never meant for it to happen, it just did. Von knew. I felt it in my soul that he did. I couldn't face him though, so I didn't."

"What happened with the case – you know anything about that?"

"Which one?"

"What'chu mean – there's more than one?"

"Yeah. When J-Prince got killed, it went cold for a while, but when Trina got killed and Von took the rap, Tinky felt safe enough to go to the police and tell them she would testify against Von, if they prosecuted Paul as well. But it didn't get that far. Von decided to plead guilty if they agreed to let Paul go."

"I thought Trina and Von was together?" Flukey was confused.

"They were. See, what people don't know is that Von used her to set up J-Prince, but they didn't expect her to be in the car that day. P killed her. Von saw to it that J-Prince went down as well. Trina's murder was put on Von, because before she died at the hospital, she told them Paul did it."

"So, why was Crazy so hell bent on getting back at Paul?" Flukey slipped up and asked.

"What'chu mean – Crazy was trying to get back at him? You think Crazy had something to do with him getting killed?" Goldy asked.

"Hell nawl, they just didn't see eye to eye," Flukey said, trying to clean it up.

"That's because P was fucking Gwen. But what a lot of people don't know is that P put her up to something."

"Something like what?"

"Flukey, keep my name out of this once I tell you."

"I will."

"P convinced Gwen to go to this police dude that liked her, and tell him that she knew about a murder. He eventually had her put a tracker on his car and place wire taps all over their house. P made it as to where everything lined up with the murder on J-Prince. He tried to make Crazy go down for it, and at first it all went as planned, but as we both know... Crazy is out and free. I'm not surprised Gwen and P ended up dead."

Goldy knew a lot, and she kind of filled in the blanks that King Von hadn't.

"You know who this girl is?" Flukey pulled up Keana's Facebook page. He had an idea about what was going on now.

Goldy looked at the page, and at first she didn't recognize her until she scrolled through some of her posts and pictures.

"That's Tinky's daughter. I think her name is Breana or Keana... Something like that. Why?"

"I just need to know what I'm getting myself into."

"I don't know what's going on, but for this shit to come back up, it can't be nothing good. Flukey, my son don't know about any of this. I want to keep it that way. And do me a favor – look out for him. Juvy really look at'chu like a brother – probably even as a father. I chose drugs over being a mother to him. You're basically all he has."

"I'll do what I can."

Flukey kind of felt bad because she had no idea what was going on with Juvy. He was stuck between a rock and a hard place – truly. The move with Keana all made sense to him now, and things were only getting worse. Crazy's word was valid in terms of what came from King Von, but Flukey was still missing something. Suddenly, Flukey got a text: 'Meet me at the trap ASAP.' It was from Crazy.

Flukey turned his attention back to Goldy.

"Juvy's a smart kid. I'm sure he's one of the few people that anybody would have to worry about."

"I know. He's just different now. I feel like he's too far into the streets to make it out of them alive."

"Maybe, but you just have to let him figure his own shit out. Besides, it's not like any of us have a choice. Juvy has to help himself. The streets don't come with a guide or how-to manual. It's something you figure out as you go," Flukey replied, then told her he had to run.

$$$$$

CRAZY

Crazy called Starskie, and put another one of his plans in motion. This was a dangerous game indeed, but it was also deceptive. You had to do what you had to do in order to get ahead, and sometimes that was by any means. He had played by the rules for a long time and that got him nowhere. Fuck that! Crazy wanted to change that. He'd spent a lot of years in a cage for sacrificing, now it was time for others to do the same.

"Once we conclude this business transaction, we can call it even, then go our separate ways," Starskie said to Crazy.

"I think that's fair. Don't drop the ball on this, because if shit goes south, I'm the one that'll have to deal with the backlash."

"As long as you put it where you say it's gonna be, I'll put it on the Search Warrant, and the judge will sign off on it. Then, we'll pick him up. Hopefully, it can all be done at the same time."

"That sounds good to me."

Crazy hung up and walked upstairs to inform the guys of what was going on. Premo was at a loss for words, as was Chris and Double. All the guys were for that matter. Juvy was like their lil' brother, and for him to be a rat was heartbreaking. They'd all went on drills with him before, so each of them could easily be hanging in the balance. Juvy could be setting them all up to go to prison for the rest of their lives.

"Shit, Crazy, I still can't see Juvy being no snitch."

Premo was having a hard time believing it. He was the one that had brought Juvy up the hill to begin with.

"Well, believe it, because it's true. I bared witness with my own two eyes," Crazy assured him. "Now everything is compromised. Juvy's been sitting on this bitch and there's no telling what he done told her. And when it come to the safety of the King, we can't chance it," Crazy added.

"It's all bad," Chris said, and shook his head in disbelief.

"Flukey might not take this laying down, and there's no telling how it will play out," Romy said, knowing how close the two of them were.

"This Nation business, and the personal shit gets set aside. If Flukey don't oblige, then other measures will be set in place. Chris, I know that's your brother and all, but we're all Black Disciples. We're your brothers, too," Crazy explained, and Chris nodded in agreement.

There was no turning back from it. Flukey was a Board Member, and if he went against what was sanctioned by law, then it could be him on the other end of the stick as well. Once you're considered to be an enemy of the people, then all bets were off. It was open season on your head.

"So, what's the plan?" Premo wanted to know.

"Juvy got to go – and the bitch. Both of them are liabilities. I hate to make a call like this, but it has to be made."

"What has to be made?" Flukey asked, as he walked through the door.

"Juvy. He want us to kill Juvy," Romy said, hoping there was something Flukey could do to put an end to the madness.

"Ain't nobody killing nobody. We don't know for sure if Juvy even told the man shit. Crazy, you can't sanction that," Flukey spoke.

"Actually, I can. If anything come in-between the safety of Von, I can make that decision. My word law. I come with King Von's word from the joint. You've already verified it. What, you didn't think I would find out you've been talking to Yatta, and that he set up a call between you and Von? I know that shit because I get my orders straight from the King himself. His word is sanctioned through me."

Flukey knew he was right, but he still would try to save Juvy's life.

"So, what, we kill Juvy, and what then? We don't have enough information to say he snitched," Flukey argued.

"Explain why he had Detective Jones' card in his pocket then? The same nigga that locked Von up," Crazy said.

What a lot of people didn't know, was that when Detective Jones was a plain clothes officer, he worked in gang-intel and had helped take down King Shorty and other high-ranking Black Disciples. Therefore, his track record with the Mob wasn't good. King Shorty put a bounty on his head, but instead of Jones being found dead somewhere, King Shorty got indicted for Conspiracy to Commit Murder and Murder for Hire. To sum it all up, Detective Jones was bad news.

"Wait, Juvy had this nigga's card in his pocket?" Premo asked, taken aback. He looked at Flukey for answers. Premo was a Board Member as well.

"Yeah, I found it," Flukey sounded defeated as he told them the truth.

"That's foul. Juvy got to go. I hate for it to come to this, but he knows too much," Premo sided with Crazy.

That definitely sealed Juvy's fate. This was the business. If things couldn't be curved for P, then there wasn't nothing in the world that could save Juvy. He was now on borrowed time and didn't even know it. This was it.

"Reach out to the lil' nigga and tell him to meet you somewhere only the two of you know about. You deal with him, and I'll get the bitch. That's what it is," Crazy said, then walked out of the room.

This is the part of the streets that turns sour and leaves you at a loss for words. There's really no way to express some things that go on beneath the hood of this machine to keep it moving forward. Blood spills over into uncharted territory and leaves an awful stench behind. Some shit you just never get used to.

It's one thing to kill a friend, but killing a brother – that changes the narrative for the worse. I still don't get how God comes up in so many conversations in the streets, especially amongst the niggaz who are putting motherfuckers in the ground. God ain't never did shit for me, so if I die today, don't let no preaching-ass nigga do my eulogy. Instead, just remember me for being...me!

CHAPTER 10

JUVY

You can always tell when something bad is about to happen. You get a gut feeling warning you to stay away, or to keep your eyes peeled.

I felt so disconnected from my senses that it was hard for me to focus; almost as if I was having an out-of-body experience. I think my biggest flaw was misplacing my loyalty and trusting the wrong niggaz. I did a lot of that. I had no idea who I was, and for the most part, I feel as if that's why I was so open to being controlled and used by other people. It gave me a purpose. I allowed others to dictate their demands and control me. Control me in ways that had destroyed my will, and destroyed the little bit of good that was left inside of me.

If I could do it all over again, would most of the decisions I've made be done differently? That's a good question. Honestly though, I think I wouldn't change a thing because hindsight is a motherfucker. Reality and perception often clash when it comes to perspective. I have no regrets. I try not to live with them, or beat myself up about bad calls made in the act of pursuing the cause. It is what it is....

The rain came down in a pour. Thunder and lightning illuminated the night skies as mother nature released her wrath. Debris and high winds carried chills throughout the eerie night and made everything seem out of place. There was no tranquility, nor calmness grounding the night. Just mystery and dark clouds.

Chicago was a dangerous city, and the murder rate was at an all-time high. Bodies were dropping all around the city. Things were bad, and Juvy had never thought it would come to this – especially with Flukey. He promised Keana that once he finished this chapter of his life, he would be done with the streets for good.

Juvy was going to kill Crazy; he *had* to die. He reached out to Flukey and said he wanted to talk, but only to him. He still felt as if Flukey had his best interest at heart. After all, he didn't do anything wrong, and he was going to explain that to him. Flukey told him to meet at their spot – a junk yard on the low-end of the southside near the Rosenwald. They would often use the junk yard to get rid of cars and other incriminating evidence they used in crimes.

Juvy walked up the street and looked around to make sure he wasn't being followed. For some reason, it felt like he was being watched.

The rain had let up by the time he made it to the meet. He climbed onto a van and jumped the gate, then headed around to the rear of the junk yard. Flukey flicked the head lights on and off when he spotted him. Juvy got inside the car and took his hood off. Flukey was drinking a bottle of Remy, which was odd because he wasn't a drinker.

"What's up, big bro?"

"Wassup Juvy? I ain't gon' lie, I wasn't going to show up, and you know why. There's a lot of shit going on, and I don't know who to trust."

"I'm not a rat, and you know that. To hear you, out of all people, say you can't trust me, hurts. I've been nothing but loyal to you, and I stand by that today. Crazy came home and fucked everything up – that nigga can't be trusted."

"What did you tell him?"

"Tell who? What the fuck you talkin' 'bout?"

"Detective Jones. I found his card in your pants pocket. How do you explain that?"

"I told you what happened. I met with the preacher from the church. That's the truth. The only thing I didn't speak on was him trying to introduce me to his friend, which was the detective. I told him I didn't want to meet the nigga. The detective gave me his card and I put it in my pocket, then left. I didn't think nothing of it. I took off. I didn't tell that man shit. He was trying to get me to talk to him about changing my life and shit – that's it. I swear to God, B!"

Juvy was hurt. He couldn't believe Flukey was thinking that way about him.

"You should have come to me, lil bro. Now my hands are tied," Flukey said, and took another drink from the bottle.

"I see. I'm a liability, huh? So, what now – you gon' kill me?" Juvy had tears swelling in his eyes.

Flukey couldn't look him in the face. This was wrong, but it was how the game was played. You have to make decisions you're against all the time. Black Disciple wasn't built on principles of personal feelings. It was always business, nothing personal. This was one of those moments. Flukey knew what he'd signed up for a long time ago. His loyalty wasn't to Juvy, it was to the Mob first.

While Juvy was talking and fighting back his tears, the passenger door opened and Crazy had one of the guys snatch Juvy out the car. He found himself surrounded. When he tried to get to his feet, he got kicked in the side. Juvy remembered the dream he had when he was pulled from underneath the van and surrounded by his assailants. The only difference was that those were his rivals, and these were his brothers.

It started to rain again and Juvy decided fighting wasn't worth it. It was inevitable, so he gave in to it – he was tired and ready to get it over with. "Do it!" he yelled, looking at Crazy.

Crazy smiled and pulled a gun from the small of his back.

"Rats don't have no place amongst this family. Get him up and take him to her," Crazy said.

Juvy was confused. Who was he talking about? They drug him over to an old sedan. Juvy looked on in suspense through blurry eyes. One of the men opened the trunk, and what Juvy saw made his knees buckle. He broke down and cried out in agony and shame. God had forsaken him for the last time. There was nothing worth living for anymore. This was it. Juvy turned to Flukey.

"I didn't do it, bro, I didn't say a word," Juvy cried.

Flukey raised his gun. "I'm sorry."

BOOM!

BOOM!

Instantly, a hole appeared in Juvy's head that spilled blood onto the concrete, and another hole caved in his cheek. Flukey wiped the tears that fell from his eyes and turned to face Crazy.

"I practically raised him, and I just took his life. You better be right about this."

187

Flukey handed Crazy the gun, then walked out of the junk yard. Crazy had Juvy's body tossed into the trunk of the car next to Keana's. Apparently, she was no longer needed, and King Von wanted her erased from the picture.

This was the ugly side of the game. There was no in-between when it came to decency. There is no loyalty and no love in this culture. Blood was often spilled, and carnage carried those trapped between good and bad. Juvy's death was tragic, as was Keana's. But this isn't it; this story is far from over with.

In fact, this is just the start of another...

If I die today, just remember me tomorrow...

(SPECIAL SHORT EDITION)

PROLOGUE

My mind went blank when I first heard my bro Dre got killed. I just couldn't believe it. I remember thinking, *How could the Mac be dead? I was just with bruh last week!* All of our plans had come together and were flourishing beyond what we could've ever imagined. And to top it off, we were just getting started.

In a way I blame myself because I had Dre go out to KC in an effort to expand our enterprise by linkin' up with Fat Tone; the same way I sent the Mob Figgaz to Ohio to link with Ampichino. Many things about Dre's death bothered me, but the questions that burned within the most were; who and why? The Kansas City press and police had formed their own theories about what had happened; but the streets talk, and The Mob was gettin' different information.

We had already found out who ordered the hit; it was most definitely Fat Tone. Everyone from the streets knew Fat Tone was a hitter out there in KC. That was one of the main reasons I wanted to tie him into The Mob's operations.

But Fat Tone fucked up: he took out a family member. In other words, he signed his own death certificate and instantly became a dead nigga walkin'.

Now that we knew who called the hit, the task at hand was to find out who the trigger man was. Word on the streets was that Fat Tone had felt Dre'd overstepped his boundaries in Kansas City and they had an exchange of words. We received different variations of what these words were about, but the cause and content of them were irrelevant: Dre was a Bay boss and his death wouldn't go unanswered. The whole Mob was ready to kill any and everybody who has anything to do with it.

Fat Tone sent word denying that he and his goons had any involvement with Dre's death, but none of that was flyin' with The Mob. Our research gave us the answers we were looking for. The fact was, we had multiple sources that gave us the same script about who was responsible for Dre's death, and when it comes to The Mob, you take one of ours, you'll be lucky if we only take two of yours....

CHAPTER 1

1986...

Everybody always asks me how I got the name "PaperBoy", or why I go by PaperBoy. PaperBoy is a name I got way back in the day, when I was only ten years old. I come from extreme poverty and grew up in a little city in The Bay called Pittsburg. These days, Pittsburg is better known as "The P", or "P World."

I was raised in the 80s. We consider those days "The Crack Era". Back then, the streets of The Bay Area were flooded with crack rock. It was to the point that, in the Projects, everybody's momma and daddy was a smoker. Mine was no exception. She was hooked! Because of this, we had it bad. By "we" I mean my lil bro and lil sis, as well as myself.

Now, some of y'all may be too young to remember when food stamps came in booklets and were "bills", like cash. Back in my day, though, that's how it was. These days, food stamps go straight onto EBT cards. This is because, in the 80s, D-Boys started accepting food stamps as payment for dope. Mind you, since food stamps weren't real "cash money", D-boys would only accept them at half price. So a five dollar rock would cost a smoker ten dollars' worth of food stamps, feel me?

That's how the game worked back then. So D-boy's didn't only have stacks of real money, they also had stacks of food stamps. And when I say stacks of food stamps, I mean fat stacks! Believe it or not, food stamps were such a factor in the dope game, even the plug would accept them when the block bleeders came to re-up!

In the hood, most of the crackheads were on welfare. Especially the single mothers. The addiction was so strong that obtaining the drug would come even before feeding their children or paying the bills. So as soon as they would get their food stamps, they would go to straight to the dope man and start spendin'.

The government knew this was a problem they had to solve, so they eventually tried doing so by putting food stamps on EBT cards. Now, that might have put a speed bump in the game, but it didn't stop nothin' because, every time a D-boy needed some groceries, the crackhead would make it happen!

Anyway, around the first of every month, my momma would get her food stamps and go straight to one of the dope boys on our block. She wouldn't blow it all on rock, though, she would grab some groceries for the house – mostly Top Ramens. But with three kids in the house, that Top Ramen, and whatever else we had to eat, wouldn't last very long. Halfway through the month, the fridge would be empty and the cupboards bare. That's where I came into play. As the oldest, I felt it was my responsibility to make sure my younger siblings didn't go without, so I'd jump off the porch and hit the streets.

At ten years old, there were not many kids my age runnin' the streets, so naturally I hung around the older crowd. They knew my situation. In fact, they were the ones serving my momma crack. These older niggas looked at me like a little brother and welcomed me up under the wing of El Pueblo Mob, aka The Lo Mob.

I remember being out on the block with the older cats, posted up, when my mom would slide through to get her rock. She would get her fix, then say somethin' slick like, "Y'all betta be takin' care my boy out here!" To which they'd reply with somethin' like, "Oh, you know he always gon' be good out here wit us!" Then my momma would smash off to get high....

CHAPTER 2

At first I'd do whatever I could to make money, such as steal bikes and sell them. Once I stole a leaf blower from a city worker's truck and would blow leaves off yards for five dollars each. Shit, I'd even rob the water fountain at the police station for all the change and cash it had in it. I was a natural hustla, so I'd always find ways to make money.

I remember one time I saw a box of pit bull puppies outside the local market. Some guy was givin' them away, free. I approached him and asked if I could have the whole box. He thought I was jokin', laughed and asked if I was serious. "Hell yeah I'm serious, I want the whole box," I told him. Once he realized I wasn't jokin' he asked if my mom would be OK with me bringin' a whole box of puppies to the house. I told him straight up: "I'm not goin' to keep 'em, I'm gonna sell 'em!"

He nodded his head as he took this in for a second, then said: "I respect that. They're all yours."

I carried the whole box home with a big-ass grin on my face because I knew I was 'bout to make some money. I already knew where I'd sell them, I just had to figure out how much I could actually get for each one. I had no idea what they went for, so I decided I'd ask for twenty dollars each.

The next day I took the puppies to the city park, which was in the next hood over – Park Side. It was baseball season and the park was flooded with people. This is a big-ass park with about six or seven baseball fields, three parking lots, a basketball court, two playgrounds, and a mini stage that can be used for a number of things. During the day the park looks nice and friendly, but don't let that fool you. During the night, the police won't even go there unless they absolutely have to.

Anyway, I hit the park with about eight pups. I knew they were pits, but I didn't know what kind of pits they were until I asked someone if he wanted to buy a pit and he said, "Oh, you got you some red noses, huh? How much you want?" I told him twenty dollars and he said "Sold!" Then he grabbed an all-white female and said he was gonna name her Remy.

I ended up sellin' all of 'em for twenty bucks each in about forty-five minutes or so. Now, that might not seem like much to you, but to a ten-year-old kid from the ghetto, I was ballin'! Not for long, of course; my money always went straight to buying food and paying bills for the house. Not that I minded; shit, that's the reason I was out there hustlin' in the first place. Besides, I really didn't have much of a choice. I can't even begin to tell you how many times our water or power was turned off, or we ran out of food. It seemed like every other month. I remember jumpin' over the fence into the neighbor's backyard and runnin' an extension cord to the outlet in the back of their house. To this day I wonder if they ever figured it out. On those months, their electric bill had to be sky high!

Regardless, no matter what, I always did my best to make sure the bills were paid and there was somethin' on the table for my little bro and sis. However, in the few times I wasn't able to make somethin' happen, and times got real bad, my mom would step up to the plate. I remember her pushin' whole grocery carts full of food right out the store without paying. She also had a little scheme where she would go into a store, grab an expensive item, then take it straight to the customer service and return it.

She would run some drag about how she couldn't find the receipt and they would give her money. I guess you could do that one time per store, but you had to show ID. They would log you into their computer and you couldn't return anything to their store without a receipt again. She always had me with her when she'd do it, I guess to throw them off. There were times when we'd hit multiple stores in multiple cities, all in one day.

CHAPTER 3

One day I was outside, chillin, in front of my spot when my little sister's friend's mom pulled up. She was there to pick up my sister for her daughter's birthday party. The lady stepped out of her soccer-mom van and was talking to my mom about what time she'd have my little sister home. Then she asked my mom a question that caught my attention: "Do you know anybody who might be interested in doing a paper route in this area?" I guess there was too much violence in the neighborhood and people kept quitting.

I instantly butted in: "I'll do it." My mom and the lady looked at me like I was crazy. I paid their looks no mind and kept going. "I can do it on my bike."

The lady smiled at me and said, "I wouldn't mind, I really need to find someone to do it, but you're too young." Then she looked at my mom: "Would you be OK with him doing it?"

My mom didn't care what I did. She knew I was in the streets all day, every day. So of course I wasn't surprised when she said, "Yeah, I would be OK with him doin' it."

The lady explained to my mom that they could make it happen as long as she – my mom – looked like the one who was actually hired on the paperwork. My mom agreed, and when the lady brought my sister home from the party, they filled out the necessary paperwork and made everything official.

On my first day, a truck pulled up and dropped off a couple stacks of newspapers, a bag of rubber bands, a list of addresses to where the papers were to be delivered, and a bag that went over my head with a pouch in the front and a pouch in the back to hold the papers while I passed them out. I didn't waste any time. I quickly started rolling papers and rubber-bandin'-'em up. When I was done, I put them in the two pouches.

I put the thing over my head with the papers, jumped on my bike and started makin' my rounds. At first I had to stop in front of every house before tossing the paper onto the doorstep. But after hittin' a few streets I started to figure out how to coast down the block and throw the paper at the same time. The trick was to hit the front door, then the paper would land right on the door mat.

While I was in the process of delivering papers, random people kept asking me if I had any extras. A few people even offered me a dollar for one. I kept saying no because I didn't think I did. But once I was done with my route I realized I did have some extras, so I backtracked looking for everyone who'd asked for one.

I was only able to find a couple of the people who'd initially asked, so I decided to start doing the asking. I was determined to sell them all, so I asked everyone I saw. I eventually sold every extra paper and made about ten extra dollars. From that day forward, I knew exactly how many extras I had, so every time someone would ask, "Do you have an extra paper?" I would respond with a question of my own: "Do you have a dollar?"

One day I was just starting to make my rounds when I ran into Kaydah. He was one of the reputable from my hood. He ended up asking me if I had an extra paper, so I asked him if he had a dollar. He started laughing and said, "OK, youngsta, I see you really are a PaperBoy."

"Yup, I sure am," I responded.

As he handed me the dollar he said, "From now on, that's yo name 'round here – PaperBoy."

Shit, he wasn't lyin' either. Next thing I knew, the whole hood was calling me PaperBoy. So by hustlin' extra papers and tryna make a few dollars, I ended up with the name PaperBoy. In fact, Kaydah was known for givin' youngstas in the hood their name. There was a whole squad of us "bay bay" kids that got our name from Kaydah. Like I said, he was a factor in the Lo. So when he gave you a name, it stuck.

Out the "squad", there were a few of us that bonded tighter than the rest. That was Rydah, Husalah, Jacka, Freako and myself. Now, we didn't all cross paths at the exact same time, but we all fell under The Mob, and linked up at some point. Ultimately, the struggle brought us to the streets, and the streets brought us together; which was the usual circumstances that came with what we call, The Game.

CHAPTER 4

By the time I was eleven, I was no longer slangin' newspapers. I had elevated to the crack game. Crackheads were always asking me if I had rocks for sale, and, well, I got tired of sendin' that money to someone else. It was time for me to get my hands on some work and start gettin' mines. I mean, it was bound to happen anyway. My family tree was known to produce hustlas. Most notably would be my uncle, Felix Mitchel, aka Felix the Cat. For those of y'all who don't know, my uncle is a legend and will forever be known as a Bay boss. He was the leader of the 69 M.O.B. (My Other Brother) in Oakland. He sold heroin until the crack era hit in the 80s, then bubbled mostly off of crack. Shit, he was bringin' in right around five million a year, then eventually got caught up and was sentenced to Life in '85. Then, in '86, some sucka killed him in Leavenworth Penitentiary, in Kansas. Gone but not forgotten, the hustle that ran through his veins, runs through mines.

One thing I heard over and over while growin' up was how much I reminded everybody of my uncle. Although I was too young to realize it, at eleven years old, I was already walkin' in his footsteps. I had set my mind on sellin' crack, and once I set my mind to somethin', ain't no stoppin' me.

So here I was, on a mission to come up on a bundle I could flip. I was choppin' it up wit' my boy Nell on the way home from school when I told him: "These smokers keep tryna buy rock from me, so I'm tryna come up on some."

He looked at me all funny, and in a whisper said, "I can get you some."

There was literally nobody around, but I still whispered back, "How? Can you get it right now?"

He explained how he was snoopin' around his dad's room and found a stack of shoeboxes full of rocks in the closet. He said he could snatch some and his dad would never know. That next mornin' I was waitin' for him in front of my spot so we could push to school together. I was waitin' and waitin' but he wasn't showin' up. I figured he chickened out, so I headed off.

I was halfway down the block when I heard my name called. I looked back and saw his ass walkin' towards me hella fast. I turned around and headed back towards him, wondering if he had brought anything. When we met up, he handed me an ice cream wrapper with five rocks inside of it, then started lookin' around all nervous and shit.

I quickly went back to my house to hide the bundle in my room, and when I came out, Nell looked a lot calmer. After school I went straight home, grabbed the bundle, jumped on my bike and hit the streets. At the end of my block I saw a tomboy named Kendra.

She was always out there gettin' money, night and day. I headed her way.

When I pulled up on her, she was smokin' a blunt and had Too Short's *Born To Mack* slappin' out her boom box. Through an exhale she said, "What you want, PaperBoy?"

I smiled as I blurted out, "I got some rocks, can you sell 'em for me?"

Through another exhale she said, "Lil boy, you ain't got no damn rocks." So I just pulled out the ice cream wrapper and handed it to her.

She grabbed it, looked at the rocks inside and handed it right back. She hit the blunt a couple more times without saying anything, then she finally said: "Check it out, PaperBoy. In these streets, you gotta get yo own money."

I instantly felt stupid. I don't even know why I asked her that in the first place. "Alright, that's what I'ma do," I told her.

I was posted on the block with Kendra for a cool minute listenin' to the Too Short tape, then a basehead came slow-draggin' up. I looked at Kendra and she said, "Go 'head, that one's you." I'd been around long enough to know how it worked, so when he got closer I hit him up.

"What you lookin' for?"

The basehead looked back and forth between Kendra and I and said, "A nickel piece." I pulled out my ice cream wrapper, did the transaction and he was gone.

After he left, Kendra gave me some game on keepin' a few rocks in my mouth under my tongue and the rest hidden elsewhere, away from where we were at. She said: "If the pigs pull up trippin', swollow 'em." After I told her I understood she went on about how I would have to throw them back up after the pigs left. She explained that I might even have to drink milk to make 'em float in my stomach, that way they'd come back up easier.

I just shrugged my shoulders and said, "I can do that."

CHAPTER 5

Being that I was way too anxious to get money, all that standin' around waitin' for baseheads wasn't workin' for me, so I jumped on my bike and told Kendra: "I'ma go find me some smokers."

She started laughin' and said: "That's right, boy. Get on yo' paper chase then."

I rode around, pullin' up on anyone who even resembled a crackhead. Before I knew it, all my rocks were gone. Shit, it couldn't have taken me longer than an hour.

Once I was out of work I headed back to the block. I pulled right back up on Kendra and said: "I got 'em off."

She looked at me with a confused look on her face. "All of 'em?" she asked.

"Yup, all of 'em."

She smiled in approval with her gold teeth on full display and said, "OK, PaperBoy. Get out there and get it then."

I started tellin' her how I'd pulled up on every knock I'd seen when she interrupted and me and asked, "So, you ready for a double-up, right?"

"What's a double-up?" I asked.

She explained that, whatever amount of money I spent, I would get enough rock to double it. I couldn't believe my ears, of course I wanted to double my money! I pulled the twenty-five dollars out my pocket, and as I handed it to her I said, "You betta know I want a double-up!"

She grabbed the money, ran into her spot and came out with my next bundle. I got on my bike, but before I smashed off to grind I said, "So we can do this double-up every time?"

"Hell yeah," she said. "And before you know it, you'll have enough to cop a real sack." With that in mind, I peeled off in search of some more baseheads.

I took School Street and headed towards the city park. When I got there I saw a couple of crackheads walking through the parking lot. They were headed towards the train tracks so I sped up and headed their way. I pulled up on them with a skid, unexpectedly, which caused them to jump. I could tell it had irritated them, but I didn't care.

"Y'all need some rock?" I asked.

They awkwardly looked at each other, then back at me. "Yeah, lil man, we do. How much you got?"

I should've known better, but answered, "I got ten rocks"

Before the words fully escaped my mouth, one of the smokers snatched me off my bike, and the other ran through my pockets.

"I'ma get y'all crackheads! Y'all just watch!" I said as they walked off with my bundle. They both just laughed as they crossed the tracks, going towards the Dime block.

I smashed back to the hood as fast as I could. When I got there, I seen Kendra, Kaydah, and a few other cats. I slid up completely out of breath: "Some punk-ass crackheads just jacked me for my bundle!"

Kendra erupted in laughter. When she finally stopped laughin' she said to Kaydah, "See? I told your PaperBoy's lil ass was out here pitchin'."

Kaydah didn't think anything was funny. "Where they at?" he asked, with his mean mug on. I explained that they'd crossed the tracks, headed towards the Dime. All he said after that was "Jump in!" We jumped into Kayda's Box Chev five deep as he gassed off slappin' "Let's Slide" by The Click.

We floated down School Street, busted a right on Railroad and went down town. We pulled up to the light, made a left on 10th street (the Dime), and another quick left towards the other side of the tracks. We coasted down the block, bent a right and I spotted them. "There they go!" I yelled.

Kaydah slid right up on them and all four doors flew open. The crackheads froze up, and before they knew it, they were surrounded. They both looked at me and knew exactly what time it was. The one that ran through my pockets dug into his and pulled out my bundle. He must've known the big homie because he said: "'Ey Kaydah, I didn't know the kid was wit you, man."

Kaydah grabbed my bundle with one hand, slapped the smoker with the other and said: "Now you do."

As soon as Kaydah slapped the first one, Kendra punched the other, then all five of us stomped they bitch-ass out.

CHAPTER 6

1993...

I remember my 17th birthday like it was yesterday. I was on my way to the homie Dirt's house in my new whip, slappin' "Young Black Brotha." My new whip was a 1981 Box Chev sittin' on Ds. Back then, if you was ridin' on Ds, you was shittin.' I'd recently copped the whip from some mark-ass nigga that I sold weed to. He'd got caught slippin' while puttin' air in the tires at a gas station. Some cats he had funk with ran up on 'im wit a banger and peeled him for his whip. A few days later, he found it with all the windows busted out.

At the time I wasn't even drivin' yet so I had to get a ride to take dude a half ounce of bomb. When I got there I saw the whip with no windows and asked him what had happened. That's when he mumbled how he got jacked for his shit. Now, I know dude had a lil paper, so I asked him why he didn't put windows in. He told me he didn't want to get caught slippin' again now that his opps knew his car, so he wanted to sell it.

As soon as I heard that I asked who his opps were and found out they were some cats I had funk with, too. I just shook my head, then said, "Fuck it, sell it to me. I'll slide in it."

Since it didn't have any windows, I ended up gettin' it for the low. The next morning I slid to the window shop to get new windows put in. Now, I was eatin' a lil bit, but it's not like I was dumb ballin', so I only put the front and rear windows in. I wasn't trippin' on the others, because I'd found someone that was sellin' some Ds. So it was either get all the windows, or only get the front and rear, but also the Ds. Of course, I did the sensible thing: I got the Ds!

Being young and wild, you know I had to stunt wit some Ds on my shit. Besides, it was summer, so it just looked like the other windows were rolled down.

I needed a blunt, so I went to the hood spot where they knew me and didn't card me. As I pulled into the parking lot I heard somebody slappin'. I looked over and saw that it was a black Honda that was also pullin' into the parking lot. Now, this was a plaza, with a bunch of little stores and a grocery store. The Honda went and parked in one of the grocery store's parking spaces.

Being that I used to steal shit from cars, I knew all I needed was a flat head to pull the window back and unlock the door. After that I could pop the trunk with the release latch and snatch the beat.

The temptation was too much. The only thing my whip was missin', besides a few windows, was some slap. I had to get 'im.

I watched as the car parked. Then some Asian cat got out and walked into the grocery store. One thing I know is, no one is in and out of a grocery store, which meant I had some time to work with.

I pulled into an empty parking space next to the Honda. I bounced out, hit the lick, and in about two minutes had some beat for my shit. I went home, hooked my shit up and was really feelin' myself.

So like I was sayin', it was my birthday and I was on my way to the homie Dirt's house in my "new" whip. He was throwin' a party that night and wanted me to come through. Dirt was from the West. I'd met him out there a few years back while stayin' in a homeless shelter called "Love A Child." We had gotten evicted, and with nowhere else to go, we ended up in that shelter. During that time I'd met a few cats, but me and Dirt really clicked.

CHAPTER 7

I pulled up to Dirt's, bounced out, tucked my pistol and dipped in. There was a gang of hoes dancin' to Too Short; a few cats I knew and a few I didn't. I stepped in dumb fresh from my hat to my shoes, so you know I had bitches peepin'. There was one, though, that was all the way locked in on me, big-ass smile and all. She was fly herself, so you know I had to smile and flash the gold ones.

I went to holla at Dirt. He wished me a happy birthday, then passed me a blunt and a bottle. As I was talkin' to bruh, I noticed ol' girl makin' her way over. I ended up meeting her half way and introduced myself. She was a thick Mexican chick with bright green eyes. She said her name was Abby.

We chopped it up real quick, but as I was walkin' off I seen some cat push up on her, lookin' mad as hell. I thought it was funny because I figured it was his bitch, but I knew I was gonna snatch her. Dirt knew it, too, and was shakin' his head with a smile as I walked back over.

I asked Dirt what was up with Abby and dude. He told me dude's name was Marv, and that Abby had him sprung. As the night went on, I noticed Marv had Abby cuffed up next to him on the couch. I also noticed how she kept lookin' my way so I said, "What you stuck on that couch fo'? Come kick it, enjoy yo' night." She hopped up instantly and strolled over next to me.

As soon as she did this, Marv got up, sent a mug my way and left. I couldn't do nothin' but laugh at dude; besides fuck his bitch, of course. The way she was all up on me, it was just a matter of time before that happened. Every time I looked into her eyes, she looked right back into mine like she wanted it right then and there.

We were on the couch flirtin' and shit, but it was time to turn up the heat. I said in her ear: "I'ma fuck yo' sexy-ass all night tonight." She responded by jumping on my lap and kissing me. She must've felt my dick get hard because she started slow grindin' on it. I could feel her breathin' harder while she kissed me, so I knew I had that pussy wet.

Out of nowhere the front door opened up. Who walked in? You guessed it, Marv; just in time to see his girl on me. She got off my lap and sat down at my side. Everybody got quiet. Marv looked at me like he wanted drama, so I bounced up on him.

"Sup, nigga?" I said.

Now, I'm far from the type to funk over a bitch, but I can't help it if the next man wants to work with emotions over one and go there with me. All I know is, he better be ready for what he's gonna have comming.

Dirt seen what was going on and pushed up on Marv: "Hold on, bruh. Yo' bitch chose up, you gotta let that go."

That's when Marv made the horrible mistake and said: "Fuck that bitch, and that bitch-ass nigga." Off pure reaction I pulled my hammer out and rocked up on ol' boy wit' a cold pistol whip. He dropped instantly and I smacked his bitch-ass with the hammer a few more times.

"Alright, Paper, he done," Dirt said as he pulled me off him.

I looked at Marv and said: "You lucky I don't smoke yo' bitch ass." Marv got up, leakin', and staggered out the door.

"I'ma end up smokin' this dude," I said to Dirt.

"Naw, he don't want them problems, trust me," Dirt said.

"I hope not, 'cause I'ma end up givin' him more than he can handle."

"I already know, but he's gone, so just relax."

"Well, now I'ma go fuck his bitch," I said, smiling.

CHAPTER 8

I figured the whole situation had baby a little shook up, so I went to calm her down. I told her I didn't want to do all that, but dude crossed the line when he called me a bitch. She nodded like she understood.

"Now that it's all over with," she said, "when I think about how you handled him, it turns me on." Then she started kissing me again and my dick lifted right back up. I had all that aggression within me, so it was time to take it out on her pussy!

I pulled baby into Dirt's bathroom, whipped out the pipe, and she started suckin'. The head was incredible, but after a few minutes, I wanted to smash the pussy. She was ready for it, too, because as soon as I pulled her up, she dropped her panties. I put a condom on, bent her over the sink and slid right in.

The pussy was wet, warm, and hella tight. While I was long-strokin' baby from the back, I watched her make fuck faces through the mirror. I pounded her pussy for a solid five minutes before she started moaning so loud I couldn't even hold back anymore. I busted a fat nut that had me shakin', while my thrusts got slower, but harder. Baby stopped moanin', I stopped poundin', and we locked eyes through the mirror.

I flushed the condom, washed my dick off in the sink real quick, then got dressed. Before we walked out I said, "We ain't done yet. I'ma take you back to the spot and fuck you all night like I promised."

She bit her bottom lip. "I can't wait," she said with a sexy-ass look.

We stepped out to Dirt's crazy ass clappin' and whistlin'. I guess they heard how I had baby in there moanin'. I told bruh I'd catch him later and we headed out.

We jumped in my whip, then I looked in my rear-view as I started the engine. For some reason, I couldn't see out my back window. I looked over my shoulder and I couldn't believe it: my muthafuckin' back window was busted out. Again! I already knew it was Marv's bitch ass. Who else could it have been?

I don't know if it was because I was drunk, or what, but I just started laughing. "See what yo' man do?" I said to Abby.

"Wow... I can't believe he did that," she said.

I told her it was nothin', though, that I'd get a new one in the morning. Then we dipped to my house with a busted-ass window.

As soon as we stepped in my room, we wasted no time gettin' to it. We fucked until the sun came up: this way, that way, and this way again. I told her I was gonna fuck her all night and I meant it. Exhaustion eventually took over and we both fell out.

I didn't wake back up until one in the afternoon. The only reason I did wake up was because baby woke me up by suckin' on my dick. "Oh, shit," I said, then baby really went to town. After bustin' a fat load in her mouth, she slurped everything up. *Damn, no wonder Marv was sprung on this*, I thought to myself.

I pulled my dick out her mouth, grabbed a rubber off my headboard, then started hittin' her doggystyle. By the time I busted another nut, I was sweatin' and out of breath. Baby was a loud one, too. I'm talkin' a real screamer. I was definitely feelin' that.

All that fuckin' had me worn out, so I fired up a blunt and we relaxed. After about an hour we jumped in the shower. This is when I really noticed how sexy baby was with all her clothes off. while I was peepin' her big-ass titties and fat ass, my dick lifted right back up. Once she seen it rockin' up, she squatted down and started suckin'.

After a couple minutes of enjoying her head game, I pulled out her mouth and slid in the pussy: this time raw, with no condom on. Her pussy was great with a condom on, so you can only imagine how it felt without one. I had her pinned up in the corner of the shower, sideways, with one leg up on the ledge of the tub. I had one hand playing with her clit in a fast motion while I slowly dicked her down. This had her screamin' even louder than before. As soon as I got close to bustin' a nut, I pulled out, put it in her mouth, and she finished me off.

CHAPTER 9

As time went, I kept fuckin' on Abby. I began picking her up after work each day because she was cashin' ya boy out. She was a waitress at a restaurant called Carrol's, in Antioch, which is the next city over from the P. We weren't in a relationship or anything, we just had a good thing goin'.

Every time I picked her up from work she'd hand me the tips she made that night. She usually made right around a hundred dollars in tips, so you know I needed that. I'd pick her up, get my dough, take her home, bash her guts, then I was gone.

Eventually she earned her spot as my main bitch. I can recall the day vividly. I'd picked her up from work and she didn't hand over her tips like usual. Instead, she said, "I just got paid. Can you take me to cash my check?" I did, and when she came back out, she handed me every dollar!

I put the money in my pocket and said: "So, I've upgraded from tips to the whole check, huh?"

She laughed. "I guess so."

I thanked her and she rode around with me while I was bustin' knocks. My tank was on Egypt, so I pulled into the gas station. Before I could even get out the whip she dug in her purse and handed me another twenty dollars, from her tip money.

"Don't trip, I got it," I told her.

"No, put it in your tank."

"I ain't gonna deny ya twice."

While pumpin' my gas I thought, *I might have to make this bitch my main*. We had the conversation and I asked her if she was ready to be my lady.

"Yes," she replied.

"What if you find out I'm fuckin' wit other bitches; are you gonna trip and want to break up?"

"No. As long as I know you're mine, I'm not gonna trip."

That's what I wanted to hear. "OK, cool," I said, and we made it official.

Right after I told her we were official she slid into the middle seat and reached for my zipper. I already knew what time it was and my dick started to swell up. She pulled it out and put it in her mouth and started bobbin'. It almost seemed like she was bobbin' to the beat of the E-40 I had slumpin'. She sucked it so good we almost crashed – twice. We eventually made it to her spot, safely, and I dropped her off.

I was on my way to the freeway, stopped at a light when I saw that nigga Marv comin' out a liquor store. I instantly grabbed my .40 Glock from under the seat and flipped a bitch. He must've recognized the whip because bruh took off diggin' down the street.

CHAPTER 10

There was no way I was gonna let this sucka-ass nigga wiggle out of what he had comin'. He probably thought he was runnin' from an ass whoopin', but he'd soon find out I had other plans.

He turned down a street and I bent it sideways right behind him. Then he cut through a yard and I knew the nigga was about to start hittin' fences. I grabbed the hammer off my lap, and as soon as he went to hop a fence, I started bustin'.

BOOM! BOOM! BOOM! BOOM!

As he hit the top of the fence, he fell to the other side. Once I saw that, I knew I had to've tagged him. But about an hour later I got a call from Dirt. He told me Marv called him and told him I busted on him. That's when I knew I missed his lucky ass. Marv told Dirt to let me know he didn't want no smoke.

I laughed. I told Dirt to let Marv's scary-ass know it was on sight. "I'll let him know," Dirt said. "But why you trippin' on this level?"

I never told Dirt Marv had busted out my window, so I filled him in on the situation and let him know I wasn't playin'. Last I heard about Marv, he moved out the P. Word was he moved in with his grandma in Frisco and started reppin' Filmoe.

I always knew one day I'd catch the nigga slippin', though. I just didn't expect it to play out or happen the way it eventually did.

CHAPTER 11

1996...

By the time I was 20, I was far more advanced than the average 20-year-old. By gettin' in the game so young, I'd been schooled by older niggas for years. This allowed me to learn from their mistakes, so every move I made was sophisticated and kept me advancin' in The Game. And not only did I have hustle and street smarts, I knew the power of a bullet – all of which served me well in The Mob.

The realization that I could kill, and was willing to do whatever necessary to reach my ends, opened my eyes. I'd been obsessed with guns and the lifestyle of a drug dealer as far back as I could remember. Not having a positive influence in my household led me to the streets, where I ultimately became fully committed to The Game. It wasn't long after that that I was drafted into The Mob.

I'm a student of The Game. Like a sponge, I always soaked up everything I could. But out of all the important lessons I've learned over the years, a few stand out the most. 1) Never fuck wit niggas that are hindered by their own stupidity, or fall victim to their emotions – like love. 2) The streets are a war zone, and any type of fear for blood or death will bring you defeat. 3) The Game is about learning, advancing, stacking, and investing. 4) Out of all the different enemies I'd encounter, the pigs are the worst.

Now, at 20 years old, I was linked in with a direct connect from Mexico. I was gettin' kicks of coke dirt cheap and making a killing in the streets. I only sold to D-boys, and I never sold nothin' under an ounce. I had a strong team of go-getters who were flippin' shit quick and bringin' fast money in.

So fast, it was time to make a power move....

CHAPTER 12

Even though I never been a rapper, I've always been around the rap game, so I understood the ins and outs when it came to utilizing rap music for business purposes. By that I mean, starting a record label and using it not only to make money, but wash money.

From everything I'd learned over the years, I knew the key to my success would be to play the background and avoid the spotlight at all costs. So after getting everything up and running, my role would be to run the operation from behind the scenes.

So that was the plan: to start a record label and have a rap group. I wanted at least four or five rappers in the group. Reason being, with more artists, we could wash more money and keep everything looking legit. We'd do so by releasing group albums, solo albums of each artist, and collaborative albums with other hot artists. The more albums we released, the more money we could wash!

Finding rappers was the easy part. I had them right in my circle. I'm talkin' real street niggas that had gas, but never pursued music because they were too caught up in the streets. However, I knew once I painted a picture, like Picasso, they would jump on board.

I called up three of my Mob niggas from the Lo; Rydah, Jacka, and Husalah; and two other Bay niggas, Fed-X and AP.9. I called them to the round-table for a meeting, then, before they arrived, I put all the money I needed "washed" on the table, for motivational purposes. When they got there and saw all that money on the table, they knew the meeting was going to change their lives.

I laid out my plan, purpose, and mission. I painted the visual for the short and long-term goals. By the end of the meeting they fully understood we weren't just building a rap group, but an organized crime operation that would extend far and wide.

It was during that meeting that The Mob Figgaz was born. After everything was agreed upon, I got up and snapped a picture of them gutta-ass niggas fresh out the streets, sittin' around all that money. It was to serve as a reminder of where we came from and where we were going. That picture is ultimately what became The Mob Figgaz logo that you still see today.

In The Mob, everybody has a position, role, and purpose. All of which are beneficial to the objectives of The Mob. The Mob Figgaz were the face of the operation. They attracted the spotlight that came with the fame and fortune. Behind the scenes, however, I was the mastermind that ran the operation – as a ghost. Doing so was a must because I knew the Feds would come snoopin' around, trying to associate the label with crime. So going undetected while making the label appear clean was my number one priority.

CHAPTER 13

While the Mob Figgaz worked relentlessly on the music, I was working for a production and release plan. I had so many connections in the rap game, I decided to explore my options. In the end, I worked a deal with Sacramento rapper C-BO. For a few birds he agreed to "Present" and promote our first album. By using 'BO, it gave us an immediate buzz because we were associated with a factor in the rap game. Tupac said C-BO was his favorite rapper, and 'BO had appeared on two songs on the classic Tupac album *All Eyez on Me.*

After I dropped 'BO off his birds, I headed back to the P. I crossed the Antioch Bridge and hit highway 4 on my way to run another play. I was ridin' dirtier than a bum's fit, so you know I was doin' the speed limit. I had my Mack 11 wit' the 30 dick, two kicks of yola and about 20 bands.

Next thing I knew, I was gettin' lit up by the Highway Patrol. Ain't this a bitch!? I would've tried to see if maybe I could just get a ticket and go, but I was on probation, with no Ls, so I knew that wasn't going to work. That meant I fa sho had to take 'im on a high-speed to try and shake his bitch ass.

I decided to pull over. This would give me a head start because I would wait until he walked up to the car to smash off. I figured by the time he got to his car I'd already be in and out of traffic. My shit was hot. I had a monster under the hood.

I pulled over and cut off the engine so the pig wouldn't get suspicious, but I kept the clutch pushed in and the stick shift in first gear so all I had to do was start up and go. The pig got out, walked behind my shit, then up the passenger side. As soon as he got by the door, I fired up the engine and gassed off. Doing so must've startled the pig because when I looked in my rear-view, I seen his bitch-ass scramblin' off the ground and runnin' to his car. In a matter of seconds I was hittin' 110, easy, in and out of lanes. I could still see the pig, but he was way behind me, so I tossed the Mack and started plottin' my next move.

CHAPTER 14

One thing I learned about high speeds is, if you're gonna get away, you gotta do it quick. Otherwise, before you know it, there will be ten more pigs and a ghetto bird involved. So that was the plan. To get away quick!

I hit the Harbor Road exit in the P and made a left. As soon as I got to Railroad, there was a PPD black and white sittin' at the light. There must've been an alert out on my car already because he hit his lights instantly. Plan "A" was a no-go, but I had everything in a Gucci duffle sittin' in the back seat, so plan "B" was to shake the pigs and toss it.

My nigga Bone stayed in the area, so I hit the nigga wit' my track phone and told him to post up by the trail off Leeland. The new plan was for me to shake the K9s long enough to smash by and toss the bag so Bone could grab it and go. I told him if it worked out he'd get a kick and he was wit' it.

I was bendin' hella turns gettin' sideways and shit, while also tryna stay in the area so I could toss the duffle. I smashed down Golf Street and downshifted to bend the turn.

Halfway through the turn I must've hit the gas a little too hard because the whip lost traction and I smacked hella hard into a parked car. This was the first time I'd ever bapped a whip (and the last, for the record), and before I could even attempt to bounce out and run, the pigs were already on me with their guns drawn.

"Fuck!" I yelled.

There was nothing I could do. They had me.

I got out the whip with my hands up, laid on my stomach and crossed my feet. Then I had hella knees and elbows jammed in my back while cuffs were slapped on my wrists. As it turned out, the Highway Patrol lit me up for my tinted windows. Ain't that some shit!? I fought the case for eight months and was sentenced to 7 years Fed time for the work and the money. From what I'd always heard, even though you had to bring all your time in the Feds, the quality of time was much better.

Well, I'd soon find out.

CHAPTER 15

I was 20 years old and on my way to Lompoc, which is a well-known federal prison in California. As soon as I stepped in, niggas began to ask me where I'm from, so I let it be known I'm from the Bay area.

"Yeah, I figured you was," said one nigga. "You got some folks right over there." I pushed over and introduced myself as PaperBoy, from The Bay.

"What part?" asked a tall skinny nigga.

"Pittsgurg," I told him.

He extended his hand as he spoke: "That's what's up. I'm Dre, from Vallejo."

I knew exactly who he was. Dre was a well-known rapper from The Bay who got cracked with some of his team for conspiracy to rob banks. He even recorded an album over the phone while fighting his case in the Fresno county jail.

Dre and I chopped it up and realized we knew a lot of the same folks. We'd just never crossed paths until now.

Once I got settled in I got in contact with 'BO and The Mob Figgaz to link them and get the plan in motion. C-BO told me he wasn't going to drop the album until he knew it was a classic and worthy of his co-sign. I told him I wouldn't expect anything less. I remained in contact with 'BO and The Figgaz throughout the whole process. I also plugged The Figgaz in with my connect in Mexico and had them grindin'.

Meanwhile, Dre and I ended up clickin' on some Mob shit. We both had that "real recognize real" vibe, and within a matter of months, we became brothers behind them walls. Before I knew it, we were bouncing ideas off one another, comin' up with plans, plots, schemes, and everything else. Bruh, like me, was money motivated, so I knew he was someone I could really fuck wit'.

I had connections in every aspect of The Game, from dope to rap. Dre had a gift, and his rap career was already in motion. In fact, he'd recently released The Rompilation, right from prison. I saw this as a rare business opportunity and began runnin' Dre down on the operation I'd started with The Figgaz. I wanted to see if he was on the same page and maybe interested in jumping on board. Not only was he on the same page, he was definitely on board!

The plan was for us to start a new rap label, together, and use it to expand the existing operation. But, this label would be the 2.0 version and it would go even deeper than The Mob Figgaz operation. See, the fundamental part of the record label with The Mob Figgaz was to basically wash money. But, since Dre and I had so much time to plot and iron out our plan, this new label would not only be used to wash drug money, but to also promote the product we were making money from. While Dre handled the music side of it, I would take care of the drug portion of the operation.

I explained to Dre I wanted to use the music to promote the drug Ecstasy. Around this time, "E", or "X" was becoming the new "in" drug and was hittin' Cali slowly but surely.

I felt like, if we got ahead of the curve on this, we can dominate the market. I explained to Dre that I had a major plug on all the ingredients, pill presses, etc. Dre asked me if I ever fucked with it, and what it was like. I told him it was a party drug and it went crazy!

I couldn't believe Dre had never fucked with E before, but then he reminded me he'd been in prison the last several years.

"Don't even trip. I'ma go to visit tomorrow and I'll have my bitch bring us some in next week," I told him. He said he was wit' it, so I put it in motion and the next week my bitch brought us 20 pills. We ended up poppin' and Dre fell in love! The nigga was "on", rappin' and dancin'. We had our own little party that day.

We were ironing out the plan and I let bruh know that the first thing I needed him to do was start the label once he got out. He asked what we were going to call it, but I wasn't sure, so we decided we'd think on it. Then I explained that I needed him to have the label up and poppin' before I got out so I could do my part right out the gates. He said he would. I let him know I'd get him some E to flip, as well as give him some dough to start the new label. I was in mid-thought when –

"Damn PaperBoy, my brain is sizzled!" said Dre.

At that point, we'd been poppin' for a couple days straight. That's when a lightbulb went off in the Mac's head: "I got it!"

"Got what?" I asked.

"The name fo' the muthafuckin' label, nigga!"

He sounded excited as hell.

"Well, let me hear it then!" I told him.

He gave me a big-ass smile and said: "We gon' call it Thizz. Thizz Entertainment."

He then continued by saying that we'd call the pills "Thizzles".

"Huh?" I said as I looked at him like he was crazy. "Bruh, we gon' have to cut you off the pills."

Then he ran me down on his train of thought. He explained how after you pop you can't think because your brain is sizzled, and that "think" plus "sizzle" is "Thizzle."

I immediately understood because the shit does sizzle your brain. The thought of it reminded me of that commercial where they show an egg and say, "This is your brain." Then they show some eggs frying in a pan and say, "This is your brain on drugs." It all made perfect sense. And that's how Thizz Entertainment was born, and how E became known as Thizzles.

Once we had the name locked in, we continued to focus on the details of the plan. This was crucial, 'cause Dre only had a few months left on his bid. I wanted to make sure all the pieces were in place and our plan was fail-proof.

CHAPTER 16

A couple weeks before Dre was to parole, he came up and told me he kept catchin' some nigga muggin' him. This happens a lot when word's out that someone will be going home soon. Bitter niggas test them thinkin' they won't do nothin' for fear of fuckin' off their release date. Anyway, Dre wasn't feelin' it one bit and said he was gonna smash the nigga if he caught him doin' it again. When he said that, I thought, *Fuck that, we need you out there!*

"Look, my nigga," I told Dre. "If he keeps it up, I'll smash him."

Dre wasn't really tryna hear it, but I finally convinced him it was in our best interest. We couldn't let nothin' fuck off our plans!

The next mornin', we was at our table, choppin' game when Dre said the nigga had walked by, on the track, lightweight muggin' again. I could tell he was hot, so I told him if the nigga was still doin' it on the next lap, I'd give him the attitude adjustment he was lookin' for.

The sucka came around again and, sure enough, he was muggin'. I bounced up and pushed up on the nigga: "What's hatnin'? You got a problem?" Before he could even answer I rocked his shit. His knees buckled a bit, but he stayed standin' and swung. I side-stepped his punch and rocked him again. This time he hit the pavement. He tried to get back up, but his legs were rubber and he fell again.

I looked around to see if the guards were on us and they weren't. I told the nigga if I caught him muggin' again I was gonna stay on his ass.

"You trippin'. I don't even know what you talkin' about," he said as he looked at me cross-eyed.

By this time niggas began to gather around as if it might crack off and that got the guards' attention, so I walked off.

Before I even looked his way I heard Dre laughin' hella hard. All I could do was shake my head as I reached out to shake Dre's hand. He finally stopped laughin' long enough to say, "You crumbled his shit," then went right back to laughin'.

Some of the folks had asked what that was all about, so I filled them in real quick and everything was good.

Two weeks later, after doing a solid year together, Dre was released back to the streets. The last thing he said to me was: "I know you believe in me and I won't let you down, my nigga."

CHAPTER 17

Dre got out and went straight into the lab. He recorded what became *Stupid Doo Doo Dumb*, which he wrote most of while in prison. In 1998 he moved to Sac, officially started our Thizz label, and dropped *Stupid Doo Doo Dumb* as our first release under the new label.

A year after *Stoopid Doo Doo Dumb*, and two years into my bid, the *C-BO's Mob Figgaz* album finally dropped. It was a bit of a challenge to get five street niggas together and focused enough to complete the album, especially with me being in prison, but we got it done.

Both albums were instant hits and both labels were up and running. At that point our target markets were Sac, The Bay, and everything in between. We hit with a splash and created major waves in the West Coast rap game; not an easy thing to do considering they were both new, independent labels. But the initial buzz created an immediate demand for more music, which gave us the momentum we needed to execute our primary mission.

The long-term objective was to build a lucrative drug operation that expanded across the entire nation. In order to do so successfully, we needed other "front" businesses to help wash the large amounts of dirty money we'd have coming in. The Mob Figgaz would clean the coke money and Thizz would clean the X money, but both labels were just a starting point – a foundation to build from. As we'd grow, we'd need other businesses such as barber shops, rim shops, auto body shops, and perhaps clothing companies, too.

As The Mob, we'd eventually form alliances with other rappers and street hustlas across the country. We'd establish ourselves as the connect with the resources to take our alliances to the next level. We'd use the music portion of the alliances to collaborate, network, and create new business opportunities, using the rappers as "influencers" in their region. This would allow us to sell more music and more work throughout America's 'hoods. And, most importantly, by networking with other rappers across the country, travelling, etc., it would give us an "alibi" – a reason for all the travelling – when the Feds came around asking questions. Therefore, every time we traveled somewhere to make a drop, we'd also record a song with the local rappers that we'd immediately release to the streets. Remember: it wasn't *if* the Feds came, it was *when* the Feds came. It was just a matter of time, and we needed to be prepared ahead of time, ya dig?

However, growing the drug operation at this level would have to wait until I got out since it's my role in The Mob. Right now, the rest of the team needs to focus on making bangers for the streets and building our influence in the rap game. And if it was easy to do, *everyone* would be factors and superstars, so I needed them focused!

CHAPTER 18

2003...

I knocked my Fed time out and was back to the streets. Dre and the Figgaz had done exceptionally well, exceeding all expectations. In 2002 Dre dropped *Thizzle Washington*, and just this year – 2003 – he dropped *Al Boo Boo*. Also this year The Mob Figgaz dropped the *Mob Figgaz* album. All albums were hits and both labels were on fire!

It was all perfect timing, too. Since the music side of the operation was poppin', I could slide right in and grow the drug portion of it. It was time to expand.

With The Mob Figgaz, we were ready to start movin' kicks of coke from state to state. We had the right contacts, and the market was there. But with Thizz and the X operation, we'd have to start from the bottom.

I remember being fresh out and hearin' our music blarin' out of cars everywhere I went. If it wasn't Mob Figgaz, it was Mac Dre; and if it wasn't Mac Dre, it was Mob Figgaz. I wasn't hearing anything else! It didn't matter where I was: in traffic, at a stop light, at the liquor store, you name it! And all this did was inspire me more.

I had to utilize my Mob ties to the Asian Mafia in San Francisco to get the ball rollin' on our X operation. Through them I was able to get everything I needed – pill presses; someone to design our different "stamps," which were pictures stamped into the various types of pills, which we also used as a way to brand; and a direct source of MDMA, which, of course, is the main ingredient.

By the time the lab was up and running, the demand for thizzles was dramatically increasing. Before I knew it, we were selling out faster than you could imagine. So I had to re-vamp the operation by opening up another lab. This one was twice the size of the first and we were still selling out!

Not that I'm complaining. Trust me, it's a good problem to have. Shit, we were selling thousands of "boats" (1,000 pills) a week, all over northern California – Sac, Stockton, The Bay, and even Fresno. At first, depending on the quantity of boats purchased, we were charging anywhere between two and five stacks each.

At that time, thizz pills were going for ten, fifteen, and even twenty dollars, depending on where you were at. Every club, rave, and house party was flooded with thizzles. If it wasn't, the function wasn't poppin'. Straight up. And whoever had the thizzles at these funtions, literally had lines of folks wanting them. With Mac Dre's influence, thizzin was the thing to do.

CHAPTER 19

Now that the thizz operation was literally poppin' in Cali, it was time to expand to other states. We contacted Ampichino in Ohio and got that situation running smoothly, then it was time to tap in with the folks in Kansas City, Missouri. We'd had a relationship with them since the early 90s when JT put on Rich The Factor. Within recent years Rich had introduced us to Fat Tone, a well-respected gang boss, who also rapped. See how it works?

Once Fat Tone confirmed the high demand for thizzles in Kansas City, Dre dipped out with a few niggas from The Mob to sort out the details and make a drop. We did this at the same time Fat Tone had a show coming up, where he scheduled Dre to perform so he'd have a legit reason to be out there. Everything was coming together as planned.

$$$$

It was about 3 am Cali time and I was dead asleep when my phone began ringing non-stop. I grabbed it off the nightstand: "Yeah, what's up?"

"Bruh, Dre is dead."

CHAPTER 20

The Vallejo Times

Bay Area Rapper Mac Dre, Dead

A San Francisco Bay area underground rap star, who police say was also a member of a gang of robbers, was killed in Kansas City, MO, when a gunman shot into a van in which he was riding. Andre Hicks, 34, known as Mac Dre, was killed about 3:30 am Monday when another vehicle pulled up beside the driver's side of the van he was in and began shooting, police said. The van swerved across the highway median, across the southbound lanes and down a steep embankment. Hicks was thrown from the van, but police said he died from the shooting. The driver crawled from the wreckage and walked for help. Hicks had performed at a concert in Kansas City, Kansas, on Friday night and stayed in the area during the weekend.

Police were trying to determine a motive, Captain Vince Cannon said. Witnesses did not hear Hicks arguing with anyone and officers do not believe the shooting stemmed from road rage, Cannon said.

Hicks has recorded more than a dozen albums since 1989. In the early 1990s, police began investigating Hicks and several associates thought to be members of the Vallejo, California's Romper Room Gang, which was suspected in a string of bank and business robberies. Hicks was eventually charged in federal court with conspiracy to commit bank robbery after he and several others were arrested while preparing to rob a bank. "We were on his tail for a long time," Vallejo police Lieutenant Rick Nichelman said.

Hicks recorded raps mocking law enforcement, often naming specific officers, including Nichelman, who was a lead investigator on the case. Nichelman said some of the lyrics were reportedly recorded over the phone while Hicks was in jail awaiting sentencing. He was released from prison in 1997.

CHAPTER 21

Just thinkin' about the death of Dre brought back so many memories from the past. Especially the good ol' days, when we first met in the Feds. Back when we built our bond behind them walls, and first started forming the plan that became the foundation of the Thizz Empire. Some of y'all might be wondering how I could look back on my days of incarceration and consider them the 'good' days. I'll admit, it does sound crazy. But, crazy or not, I found myself wishing I could have those days back. At least then, the Mac was alive.

I remember when I first got out and Dre threw a huge party for me. It seems like it was just yesterday. Dre was really feelin' himself that night. He wanted to make sure it was poppin' in a real way, so everybody who was somebody in The Mob was there. Just thinkin' on it now makes me grin. Dre's wild ass was thizzed out his mind!

I can still picture him giggin' and shit with his signature 'thizz face' on. He had the whole spot live, like a concert. We had so much fun that night, it was more like a frat party than a Mob celebration. But that was Dre; he definitely knew how to live life...

My bad; I got lost in my thoughts, reminiscin'. Back to the story; them Kansas City niggas stole our brother's life, and they gotta pay for that!

CHAPTER 22

We knew Fat Tone was behind the hit. Nothin' happened in Kansas City without Tone at least knowin' about it. And after a few weeks of solid investigation, our sources confirmed as much. But we also learned Fat Tone wasn't the trigger man. Turns out, Tone sent his right-hand man, Cowboy, to do the job. In any case, they both would pay, and now that we had the necessary information, it was time to strategize our plan to hit back.

We knew with everything goin' on with Dre's death, bringin' it to 'em in Kansas City wouldn't work. The cops were everywhere, investigating, and Fat Tone and his crew knew we were trippin', so it was very likely he had his goons ready, locked and loaded, and on high alert for any outsiders. Especially Bay cats, and we fo' sho stand out.

We also knew Tone wasn't stupid enough to come to Cali. Shit, the whole Bay Area wanted Fat Tone's head, so we would have to figure somethin' else out.

Tone started reachin' out to The Mob, denying any involvement and assuring us that, whoever was responsible would pay. We did not feel the need to give him a head's up that we'd already confirmed exactly who it was; and that yes, they would most certainly pay. Instead, The Mob chose to let Tone think we believed him. We even told him the driver of Dre's van confirmed that the shooting stemmed from road rage. Nevertheless, we knew Tone wasn't stupid enough to completely let his guard down, so we decided to slow-play the situation and work on gaining Tone's trust little by little. We started by letting Tone know we wanted to continue with the drug operation, but with all the heat surrounding Dre's death, we'd have to let the chaos die down first.

$$\$\$\$\$\$$$

By mid-February, three months after Dre's death, the dust seemed to have settled, so we decided it was time to put things in motion. We contacted Fat Tone and told him we were ready to re-open up the operation. As always, we like to make things look music related, and since Mac Dre was gone, we decided to link him up with Mac Minister. Mac Minister was a "Promoter" we had stationed in Vegas, where he also owned and operated several escort services.

We needed to make sure Tone lowered his guard, so Minister's primary objective was to gain his trust, by any means necessary. I knew Minister was game tight. My only concern was that he tends to be hot headed and impulsive, so I stressed to him the importance of remaining calm, cool, and collected. He assured me there was no need to worry.

To test where Fat Tone's head was, regarding trust, we set up the initial meeting for the following month, in Vegas. We wanted to see if he'd leave Kansas City and come out west.

He did. And the initial meeting between Mac Minister and Fat Tone went even better than expected. Mac showed Tone the Vegas high life – drugs, sex, money and hoes. He took him gambling, gave him a tour of his various escort companies, then hooked him up with 50k worth of thizzles to take back to Kansas City.

Now that that went well, the next step was to assist Tone with his career in the rap game. Tone desperately wanted to be a "real" rapper, and The Mob's connections in the rap game expand far and wide. After pulling some strings, Mac Minister took Tone out to New York to meet some 'mainstream' rappers. "This nigga wants to be a rap star so bad, and I got him thinkin' he gon' be the next Pac!" Mac Minister said during a phone call we had while he was in New York.

Once Mac Minister expressed that he'd fully gained Fat Tone's trust, we decided it was time to put the actual hit in motion. I got with my bro J Diggs so we can figure out the details. After bouncing some ideas off each other we decided it was time to call a meeting wit the Family.

That Easter weekend, The Mob gathered at the round-table to strategize the most critical part of our mission: The hit!

CHAPTER 23

Everyone knows the key to develop a successful plan starts with figuring out the five Ws: Who, what, when, where, and why.

The 'who' was the hardest of them all to figure out? Niggas practically started fightin' over who would have the honors of knockin' Tone down. There wasn't a soul in the room that wasn't ready and willin'. The job was like a fish in the middle of hungry killer sharks. In the end, we settled on Mac Minister (obviously, because he was the one who'd gain Tone's trust) and a prospect who had been gettin' pulled into The Mob by Mac Dre himself. You can't get fully into The Mob without a body; what better for the young thug than to take the life of the man who killed his mentor?

The 'what' was basically a no-brainer. We would just line up another 'transaction' with Tone to lure him to a spot where we would make the hit.

The 'when' came surprisingly easy. In fact, it seemed like Minister had thought of it ahead of time. "Snoop Dogg has a concert in Vegas commin' up soon. "I can tell Fat Tone I got him plugged in to open for Snoop," he said.

"How soon?" I asked.

"Towards the end of next month. The 24th, I believe," Minister answered.

"That'll work," I said. "He already knows we like to keep everything music related, so we'll set up his next 'pick-up' at that time. Coppin' work and openin' for Snoop Dogg will get him there and have him ego drunk. We'll get it done during that time, maybe a couple days before the show."

We all agreed.

And last, but definitely not least, the 'why' was already written in blood.

The meeting with The Mob went well and the foundation for the plan was formed.

CHAPTER 24

On May 20th, a little over six months after Dre was murdered, it was time to make our move. Minister called Tone with the good news: in addition to Tone comin' to Vegas for the transaction, he would also be opening for Snoop Dogg. Tone was beyond excited.

$$$$$

On the 22nd, while Tone was on a red-eye to Vegas, the prospect was pullin' up to Minister's with his ho bitch. They slid up in her whip since it was legit, yet also couldn't be traced back to The Mob.

While they waited for Tone, they discussed specifics. Then, as customary in Vegas, the prospect put his ho bitch to work.

Once Tone was scheduled to arrive, Minister went to the airport to pick him up. When he got there, he was surprised. Tone wasn't alone: he brought his own ho bitch, as well as his right-hand man, Cowboy. *Perfect,* Minister thought to himself. *The Mac Gods are setting things up perfectly.*

When they got to Minister's spot, Minister ran Tone down on the specifics of the plan.

"I got a legit whip in my bitch's name that we use for trips. It has a secret compartment. Not only are you welcome to use it while you're out here, you can use it to transport the work back to K.C. – unless you'd rather slide in a rental," Mac told him.

Then he continued: "The transaction is scheduled to go down tomorrow night at 11:30. Same place as last time – the housing development down the street. I don't do nothin' here no mo'. My spot's been hot, wit all these nosey-ass neighbors," he said as he nodded towards a neighbor they saw lookin' in their direction.

Tone agreed and thanked Minister for everything. Afterwards, he mentioned he was gettin' a room for two at the MGM, then droppin' his ho bitch off on the blade and hittin' the town for some gambling, which he loved to do.

Minister threw Tone the keys to the under bucket. "Do what you do. I'll meet you at the MGM tomorrow night and we'll meet up wit' the connect from there," Minister said.

$$$$$

Around 10:30 the following night, Minister pulled up to the MGM. He met up with Tone and Cowboy, then they headed to the parking garage to retrieve the under bucket. All three loaded in, then made their way to the meet-up spot.

Once there, they found themselves waiting... and waiting. Minister was getting anxious and frustrated with the prospect. He should have been there already!

"I'ma call this nigga and see where the fuck he at," Minister said as he stepped out the car for some privacy. While he was talking to the prospect, who was just around the corner, he looked through the car window and saw Tone get on his phone.

After Minister hung up, he got in the car, just as Tone was ending his conversation with, 'I'ma call you as soon as I get back to the hotel.'

"This nigga right around the corner," Mac Minister said. A couple minutes later they saw headlights. Minister told Tone, "Flash your headlights so he can see where we at."

The prospect pulled up, flipped a bitch, then backed up to Tone's car with the trunks a few feet away from each other, just like they discussed previously.

"Pop the trunk," Minister said. "I'll make the swap." Then he got out the car and met the prospect between the two bumpers. He grabbed the money out of Tone's trunk, said something to the prospect, then went and set it on the back seat of the prospect's whip. Tone looked in his rearview, but couldn't see much because his trunk was up. When he looked in his side-view mirror, he saw the prospect come from behind his car and up the driver's side with a duffle bag.

This nigga finna show me the work, Tone thought to himself.

But he was wrong. Very wrong. When the prospect reached into the bag, he came out with an AK-47 with an extended clip. Before Tone's brain could even register what was happening, he saw it pointed at his face. The prospect let it rip and bullets tore through Tone's face and chest. Cowboy jumped out of the car and started running. As he reached for his waist, the prospect sent two at him, hitting him in his back. Tat! Tat! He screamed and fell.

The prospect hit Tone a few more times even though it was clear he was already dead. Chunks went missing from Tone's body as he layed slumped over. The prospect then went up to finish off Cowboy, who was in a puddle of his own blood trying to crawl away. Cowboy turned on his back and began begging for his life as the prospect pointed the K at him. Once close enough, the prospect saw a gun laying next to Cowboy – he'd dropped it when he was hit.

"Y'all thought you could get away wit' killin' the MAC?! You bitch-ass nigga! Nobody get away wit' killin' a member of The Mob!" The prospect popped Cowboy's kneecap. The K bullet damn near cut his leg in two.

"Aaaaaahhhhh! Please, don't kill me," Cowboy begged.

"You already dead, bitch-ass nigga," the prospect replied. Then he smiled and let seven more shots rip through the nigga – Tat! Tat! Tat! Tat! Tat! Tat! Tat!

"Let's go nigga!" Minister yelled to the prospect from the driver's seat of the car the prospect pulled up in.

The prospect picked up Cowboy's gun off the street, then jumped in the car with Minister. Minister sped off.

When they got a safe distance from the murder scene, the prospect opened the bag of money. It had stacks of hundred-dollar bills. However, under a few layers of bills, it had cut-up newspaper. *What the fuck?* The prospect thought to himself. Then it hit him.

"Minister, them niggas was gonna rob us!" The prospect said.

"What you mean 'rob us', nigga?"

The prospect reached under the stacks of money and pulled out stacks of paper cut the same size as money. Then he showed him the Glock he picked up off the street next to Cowboy.

Mac Minister understood exactly.

They went and scooped the ho bitch from the blade and headed to The Bay, slappin' Mac Dre the whole way.

$$$$$

THE MOB (FULL-LENTH NOVEL) AVAILABLE NOW FROM THE CELL BLOCK AND ON AMAZON!

MIKE ENEMIGO PRESENTS

THE CELL BLOCK

BOOK SUMMARIES

MIKE ENEMIGO is the new prison/street art sensation who has written and published several books. He is inspired by emotion; hope; pain; dreams and nightmares. He physically lives somewhere in a California prison cell where he works relentlessly creating his next piece. His mind and soul are elsewhere; seeing, studying, learning, and drawing inspiration to tear down suppressive walls and inspire the culture by pushing artistic boundaries.

THE CELL BLOCK is an independent multimedia company with the objective of accurately conveying the prison/street experience with the credibility and honesty that only one who has lived it can deliver, through literature and other arts, and to entertain and enlighten while doing so. Everything published by The Cell Block has been created by a prisoner, while in a prison cell.

THE BEST RESOURCE DIRECTORY FOR PRISONERS, $19.99 & $7.00 S/H: This book has over 1,450 resources for prisoners! Includes: Pen-Pal Companies! Non-Nude Photo Sellers! Free Books and Other Publications! Legal Assistance! Prisoner Advocates! Prisoner Assistants! Correspondence

Education! Money-Making Opportunities! Resources for Prison Writers, Poets, Artists! And much, much more! Anything you can think of doing from your prison cell, this book contains the resources to do it!

A GUIDE TO RELAPSE PREVENTION FOR PRISONERS, $15.00 & $5.00 S/H: This book provides the information and guidance that can make a real difference in the preparation of a comprehensive relapse prevention plan. Discover how to meet the parole board's expectation using these proven and practical principles. Included is a blank template and sample relapse prevention plan to assist in your preparation.

LOST ANGELS: $15.00 & $5.00: David Rodrigo was a child who belonged to no world; rejected for his mixed heritage by most of his family and raised by an outcast uncle in the mean streets of East L.A. Chance cast him into a far darker and more devious pit of intrigue that stretched from the barest gutters to the halls of power in the great city. Now, to survive the clash of lethal forces arrayed about him, and to protect those he loves, he has only two allies; his quick wits, and the flashing blade that earned young David the street name, Viper.

LOYALTY AND BETRAYAL DELUXE EDITION, $19.99 & $7.00 S/H: Chunky was an associate of and soldier for the notorious Mexican Mafia – La Eme. That is, of course, until he was betrayed by those, he was most loyal to. Then he vowed to become their worst enemy. And though they've attempted to kill him numerous times, he still to this day is running around making a mockery of their organization .... This is the story of how it all began.

MONEY IZ THE MOTIVE: SPECIAL 2-IN-1 EDITION, $19.99 & $7.00 S/H: Like most kids growing up in the hood, Kano has a dream of going from rags to riches. But when his plan to get fast money by robbing the local "mom and pop" shop goes wrong, he quickly finds himself sentenced to serious prison time. Follow Kano as he is schooled to the ways of the game by some of the most respected OGs whoever did it; then is set free and given the resources to put his schooling into action and build the ultimate hood empire...

DEVILS & DEMONS: PART 1, $15.00 & $5.00 S/H: When Talton leaves the West Coast to set up shop in Florida he meets the female version of himself: A drug dealing murderess with psychological issues. A whirlwind of sex, money and murder inevitably ensues and Talton finds himself on the run from the law with nowhere to turn to. When his team from home finds out he's in trouble, they get on a plane heading south...

DEVILS & DEMONS: PART 2, $15.00 & $5.00 S/H: The Game is bitter-sweet for Talton, aka Gangsta. The same West Coast Clique who came to his aid ended up putting bullets into the chest of the woman he had fallen in love with. After leaving his ride or die in a puddle of her own blood, Talton finds himself on a flight back to Oak Park, the neighborhood where it all started...

DEVILS & DEMONS: PART 3, $15.00 & $5.00 S/H: Talton is on the road to retribution for the murder of the love of his life. Dante and his crew of killers are on a path of no return. This urban classic is based on real-life West Coast underworld politics. See what happens when a group of YG's find themselves in the midst of real underworld demons...

DEVILS & DEMONS: PART 4, $15.00 & $5.00 S/H: After waking up from a coma, Alize has locked herself away from the rest of the world. When her sister Brittany and their friend finally take her on a girl's night out, she meets Luck – a drug dealing womanizer.

FREAKY TALES, $15.00 & $5.00 S/H: *Freaky Tales* is the first book in a brand-new erotic series. King Guru, author of the *Devils & Demons* books, has put together a collection of sexy short stories and memoirs. In true TCB fashion, all of the erotic tales included in this book have been loosely based on true accounts told to, or experienced by the author.

THE ART & POWER OF LETTER WRITING FOR PRISONERS: DELUXE EDITION $19.99 & $7.00 S/H: When locked inside a prison cell, being able to write well is the most powerful skill you can have! Learn how to increase your power by writing high-quality personal and formal letters! Includes letter templates, pen-pal website strategies, punctuation guide and more!

THE PRISON MANUAL: $19.99 & $7.00 S/H: *The Prison Manual* is your all-in-one book on how to not only survive the rough terrain of the American prison system, but use it to your advantage so you can THRIVE from it! How to Use Your Prison Time to YOUR Advantage; How to Write Letters that Will

Give You Maximum Effectiveness; Workout and Physical Health Secrets that Will Keep You as FIT as Possible; The Psychological impact of incarceration and How to Maintain Your MAXIMUM Level of Mental Health; Prison Art Techniques; Fulfilling Food Recipes; Parole Preparation Strategies and much, MUCH more!

GET OUT, STAY OUT!, $16.95 & $5.00 S/H: This book should be in the hands of everyone in a prison cell. It reveals a challenging but clear course for overcoming the obstacles that stand between prisoners and their freedom. For those behind bars, one goal outshines all others: GETTING OUT! After being released, that goal then shifts to STAYING OUT! This book will help prisoners do both. It has been masterfully constructed into five parts that will help prisoners maximize focus while they strive to accomplish whichever goal is at hand.

MOB$TAR MONEY, $12.00 & $4.00 S/H: After Trey's mother is sent to prison for 75 years to life, he and his little brother are moved from their home in Sacramento, California, to his grandmother's house in Stockton, California where he is forced to find his way in life and become a man on his own in the city's grimy streets. One day, on his way home from the local corner store, Trey has a rough encounter with the neighborhood bully. Luckily, that's when Tyson, a member of the MOBTAR, a local "get money" gang comes to his aid. The two kids quickly become friends, and it doesn't take long before Trey is embraced into the notorious MOB$TAR money gang, which opens the door to an adventure full of sex, money, murder and mayhem that will change his life forever... You will never guess how this story ends!

BLOCK MONEY, $12.00 & $4.00 S/H: Beast, a young thug from the grimy streets of central Stockton, California lives The Block; breathes The Block; and has committed himself to bleed The Block for all it's worth until his very last breath. Then, one day, he meets Nadia; a stripper at the local club who piques his curiosity with her beauty, quick-witted intellect and rider qualities. The problem? She has a man – Esco – a local kingpin with money and power. It doesn't take long, however, before a devious plot is hatched to pull off a heist worth an indeterminable amount of money. Following the acts of treachery, deception and betrayal are twists and turns and a bloody war that will leave you speechless!

HOW TO HUSTLE AND WIN: SEX, MONEY, MURDER EDITION $15.00 & $5.00 S/H: *How To Hu$tle and Win: Sex, Money, Murder Edition* is the grittiest, underground self-help manual for the 21st century street entrepreneur in print. Never has there been such a book written for today's gangsters, goons and go-getters. This self-help handbook is an absolute must-have for anyone who is actively connected to the streets.

RAW LAW: YOUR RIGHTS, & HOW TO SUE WHEN THEY ARE VIOLATED! $15.00 & $5.00 S/H: *Raw Law For Prisoners* is a clear and concise guide for prisoners and their advocates to understanding civil rights laws guaranteed to prisoners under the US Constitution, and how to successfully file a lawsuit when those rights have been violated! From initial complaint to trial, this book will take you through the entire process, step by step, in simple, easy-to-understand terms. Also included are several examples where prisoners have sued prison officials successfully, resulting in changes of unjust rules and regulations and recourse for rights violations, oftentimes resulting in rewards of thousands, even millions of dollars in damages! If you feel your rights have been violated, don't lash out at guards, which is usually ineffective and only makes matters worse. Instead, defend yourself successfully by using the legal system, and getting the power of the courts on your side!

HOW TO WRITE URBAN BOOKS FOR MONEY & FAME: $16.95 & $5.00 S/H: Inside this book you will learn the true story of how Mike Enemigo and King Guru have received money and fame from inside their prison cells by writing urban books; the secrets to writing hood classics so you, too, can be caked up and famous; proper punctuation using hood examples; and resources you can use to achieve your money motivated ambitions! If you're a prisoner who want to write urban novels for money and fame, this must-have manual will give you all the game!

PRETTY GIRLS LOVE BAD BOYS: AN INMATE'S GUIDE TO GETTING GIRLS: $15.00 & $5.00 S/H: Tired of the same, boring, cliché pen pal books that don't tell you what you really need to know? If so, this book is for you! Anything you need to know on the art of long and short distance seduction is included within these pages! Not only does it give you the science of attracting pen pals from websites, it also includes psychological profiles and instructions on how to seduce any woman you set your sights on! Includes interviews of women who have fallen in love with prisoners, bios for pen pal ads, pre-written love letters, romantic poems, love-song lyrics, jokes and much, much more! This book is the ultimate guide – a must-have for any prisoner who refuses to let prison walls affect their MAC'n.

THE LADIES WHO LOVE PRISONERS, $15.00 & $5.00 S/H: New Special Report reveals the secrets of real women who have fallen in love with prisoners, regardless of crime, sentence, or location. This info will give you a HUGE advantage in getting girls from prison.

THE MILLIONAIRE PRISONER: PART 1, $16.95 & $5.00 S/H

THE MILLIONAIRE PRISONER: PART 2, $16.95 & $5.00 S/H

THE MILLIONAIRE PRISONER: SPECIAL 2-IN-1 EDITION, $24.99 & $7.00 S/H: Why wait until you get out of prison to achieve your dreams? Here's a blueprint that you can use to become successful! *The Millionaire Prisoner* is your complete reference to overcoming any obstacle in prison. You won't be able to put it down! With this book you will discover the secrets to: Making money from your cell! Obtain FREE money for correspondence courses! Become an expert on any topic! Develop the habits of the rich! Network with celebrities! Set up your own website! Market your products, ideas and services! Successfully use prison pen pal websites! All of this and much, much more! This book has enabled thousands of prisoners to succeed and it will show you the way also!

THE MILLIONAIRE PRISONER 3: SUCCESS UNIVERSITY, $16.95 & $5.00 S/H: Why wait until you get out of prison to achieve your dreams? Here's a new-look blueprint that you can use to be successful! *The Millionaire Prisoner 3* contains advanced strategies to overcoming any obstacle in prison. You won't be able to put it down!

THE MILLIONAIRE PRISONER 4: PEN PAL MASTERY, $16.95 & $5.00 S/H: Tired of subpar results? Here's a master blueprint that you can use to get tons of pen pals! *TMP 4: Pen Pal Mastery* is your complete roadmap to finding your one true love. You won't be able to put it down! With this book you'll DISCOVER the SECRETS to: Get FREE pen pals & which sites are best to use; successful tactics female prisoners can win with; use astrology to find love, friendship & more, build a winning social media presence. All of this and much more!

THE MILLIONAIRE PRISONER 5: FREE MONEY, $24.95 & $7.00 S/H: Wish you could find more FREE MONEY like your stimulus? Seeking an end to your money problems? Look no further! Here's a master blueprint that reveals all that's available! *Tmp 5: Free Money* is your complete roadmap to finding all the FREE MONEY options out there for convicts. You won't be able to put it down!

GET OUT, GET RICH: HOW TO GET PAID LEGALLY WHEN YOU GET OUT OF PRISON!, $16.95 & $5.00 S/H: Many of you are incarcerated for a money-motivated crime. But w/

today's tech & opportunities, not only is the crime-for-money risk/reward ratio not strategically wise, it's not even necessary. You can earn much more money by partaking in any one of the easy, legal hustles explained in this book, regardless of your record. Help yourself earn an honest income so you can not only make a lot of money, but say good-bye to penitentiary chances and prison forever! (Note: Many things in this book can even he done from inside prison.) (ALSO PUBLISHED AS *HOOD MILLIONAIRE: HOW TO HUSTLE AND WIN LEGALLY!*)

THE CEO MANUAL: HOW TO START A BUSINESS WHEN YOU GET OUT OF PRISON, $16.95 & $5.00 S/H: $16.95 & $5.00 S/H: This new book will teach you the simplest way to start your own business when you get out of prison. Includes: Start-up Steps! The Secrets to Pulling Money from Investors! How to Manage People Effectively! How To Legally Protect Your Assets from "them"! Hundreds of resources to get you started, including a list of "loan friendly" banks! (ALSO PUBLISHED AS *CEO MANUAL: START A BUSINESS, BE A BOSS!*)

THE MONEY MANUAL: UNDERGROUND CASH SECRETS EXPOSED! 16.95 & $5.00 S/H: Becoming a millionaire is equal parts what you make, and what you don't spend – AKA save. All Millionaires and Billionaires have mastered the art of not only making money, but keeping the money they make (remember Donald Trump's tax maneuvers?), as well as establishing credit so that they are loaned money by banks and trusted with money from investors: AKA OPM – other people's money. And did you know there are millionaires and billionaires just waiting to GIVE money away? It's true! These are all very-little known secrets "they" don't want YOU to know about, but that I'm exposing in my new book!

HOOD MILLIONAIRE; HOW TO HUSTLE & WIN LEGALLY, $16.95 & $5.00 S/H: Hustlin' is a way of life in the hood. We all have money motivated ambitions, not only because we gotta eat, but because status is oftentimes determined by one's own salary. To achieve what we consider financial success, we often invest our efforts into illicit activities – we take penitentiary chances. This leads to a life in and out of prison, sometimes death – both of which are counterproductive to gettin' money. But there's a solution to this, and I have it...

CEO MANUAL: START A BUSINESS BE A BOSS, $16.95 & $5.00 S/H: After the success of the urban-entrepreneur classic *Hood Millionaire: How To Hustle & Win Legally!*, self-made millionaires Mike Enemigo and Sav Hustle team back up to bring you the latest edition of the Hood Millionaire series – *CEO Manual: Start A Business, Be A Boss!* In this latest collection of game laying down the art of "hoodpreneurship", you will learn such things as: 5 Core Steps to Starting Your Own Business! 5 Common Launch Errors You Must Avoid! How To Write a Business Plan! How To Legally Protect Your Assets From "Them"! How To Make Your Business Fundable, Where to Get Money for Your Start-up Business, and even How to Start a Business With No Money! You will learn How to Drive Customers to

Your Website, How to Maximize Marketing Dollars, Contract Secrets for the savvy boss, and much, much more! And as an added bonus, we have included over 200 Business Resources, from government agencies and small business development centers, to a secret list of small-business friendly banks that will help you get started!

PAID IN FULL: WELCOME TO DA GAME, $15.00 & $5.00 S/H: In 1983, the movie *Scarface* inspired many kids growing up in America's inner cities to turn their rags into riches by becoming cocaine kingpins. Harlem's Azie Faison was one of them. Faison would ultimately connect with Harlem's Rich Porter and Alpo Martinez, and the trio would go on to become certified street legends of the '80s and early '90s. Years later, Dame Dash and Roc-A-Fella Films would tell their story in the based-on-actual-events movie, *Paid in Full*.

But now, we are telling the story our way – The Cell Block way – where you will get a perspective of the story that the movie did not show, ultimately learning an outcome that you did not expect.

Book one of our series, *Paid in Full: Welcome to da Game*, will give you an inside look at a key player in this story, one that is not often talked about – Lulu, the Columbian cocaine kingpin with direct ties to Pablo Escobar, who plugged Azie in with an unlimited amount of top-tier cocaine at dirt-cheap prices that helped boost the trio to neighborhood superstars and certified kingpin status... until greed, betrayal, and murder destroyed everything....(ALSO PUBLISHED AS *CITY OF GODS*.)

OJ'S LIFE BEHIND BARS, $15.00 & $5 S/H: In 1994, Heisman Trophy winner and NFL superstar OJ Simpson was arrested for the brutal murder of his ex-wife Nicole Brown-Simpson and her friend Ron Goldman. In 1995, after the "trial of the century," he was acquitted of both murders, though most of the world believes he did it. In 2007 OJ was again arrested, but this time in Las Vegas, for armed robbery and kidnapping. On October 3, 2008 he was found guilty sentenced to 33 years and was sent to Lovelock Correctional Facility, in Lovelock, Nevada. There he met inmate-author Vernon Nelson. Vernon was granted a true, insider's perspective into the mind and life of one of the country's most notorious men; one that has never been provided...until now.

THE LIFE AND TIMES OF MAC DRE, $16.99 & $5.00 S/H: *The Life and Times of Mac Dre* is an urban novel told in the voice of the Bay Area hip-hop legend as he describes his early years growing up in a California ghetto called Crest Side, in the city of Vallejo. Along the way, he encounters challenges and obstacles, leading to a thrilling journey that takes place during the crack epidemic. This memoir-styled tale depicts rapper Mac Dre's true-life experiences as he entered the music industry, became a bank robber and ultimately landed in the Federal Bureau of Prisons. With its compelling storyline and unforgettable characters, *The Life and Times of Mac Dre* is an urban masterpiece that will keep readers captivated from start to finish.

THE MOB, $16.99 & $5.00 S/H: PaperBoy is a Bay Area boss who has invested blood, sweat, and years into building The Mob – a network of Bay Area street legends, block bleeders, and underground rappers who collaborate nationwide in the interest of pushing a multi-million-dollar criminal enterprise of sex, drugs, and murder.

Based on actual events, little has been known about PaperBoy, the mastermind behind The Mob, and intricate details of its operation, until now.

Follow this story to learn about some of the Bay Area underworld's most glamorous figures and famous events...

COCAINE QUEEN (PREQUEL), $12.00 & $4.00 S/H. She was a loving mother.

She was also a ruthless and treacherous drug lord who's suspected of murdering more than one husband.

Who was she?

Griselda Blanco, the Queen of Cocaine, aka The Godmother.

From the streets of New York, to the ghettoes of Columbia, to the mansions of Miami, *Cocaine Queen: The Reign of Griselda Blanco*, is a based-on-actual-events story that takes you on a dangerous ride along the bloody rise to power of the most notorious female drug lord in history, as she kills anyone who gets in her way of complete dominance of the American cocaine market....

COCAINE QUEEN (BOOK ONE), $17.95 & $5.00 S/H.

COCAINE QUEEN (BOOK TWO), $17.95 & $5.00 S/H.

SOSA: KILLING TONY MONTANA (PREQUEL), $12.00 & $4.00 S/H. Cuban refuge, Tony

"Scarface" Montana, had one thing on his mind when he got to America: To turn his rags into riches! With the help of his best friend, Manny, he created one of the biggest, bloodiest, most vicious cocaine organizations in American history. But Tony made a grave mistake when he failed to carry out the hit on Orlando Gutierrez, a reporter who threatened the empire of Tony's boss, Bolivian drug lord Alejandro Sosa.

The consequence?

Death.

Sosa: Killing Tony Montana is the prequel to the upcoming, highly-anticipated *Sosa* saga. It details aspects of Sosa's brutal attack on Tony that the movie didn't show, such as Sosa contracting the violent hit squad of the Cocaine Queen herself, Griselda Blanco, to assist his most dangerous assassin carry out the murder, while Sosa tries to make right with his cocaine colleagues, such as Pablo Escobar, El Chapo Guzman, and the world's biggest cocaine cartel: The CIA.

SOSA: THE PRICE OF POWER (BOOK ONE), $19.95 & $5.00 S/H: The 1983 classic gangster film *Scarface* wooed over a billion fans worldwide, but it ended in the abrupt, violent massacre of Tony and his squad at the behest of ruthless Bolivian crime boss, Alejandro Sosa.

Since then, *Scarface* has birthed a nation of diehards who have been waiting decades for a Hollywood response. The wait is now over. Tony is dead, but his legacy lives inside of Elvira, who has resurfaced in the riveting masterpiece saga entitled: *Sosa: The Price of Power*. First, Sosa must scramble to pick up the pieces which were left shattered by the betrayal of Tony.

The true *Scarface* fan will be glued to the cold-blooded cunning, the bigger-than-life characters who Sosa surrounds himself with, and the skilled moves he makes on an international scale. For the blonde bombshell, the game becomes life or death. Who can't remember Tony's enemies: Gaspar Gomez, the Diaz brothers and others? They are the Miami Cuban Mafia and are hunting Elvira down for the huge nine-figure fortune her husband left behind....

SOSA: THE REIGN (BOOK TWO), $19.95 & $5.00 S/H: In book one of this mega-hit series, *Sosa: The Price of Power*, Elvira appealed to Sosa to protect her from the Miami Cuban Mafia (MCM), who were trying to force her to hand over millions of dollars left by her dead husband. Surprised but eager, Sosa sent a couple of his best assassins to Miami to neutralize the MCM and muscle them into backing off the pregnant bombshell. Now Elvira (who may or may not know Sosa had Tony Montana hit) has made a new ally and friend, but with her husband out of the picture, Sosa finds himself in need of a solid business contact inside of the USA.

With Dr. Orlando Gutierrez assassinated, Sosa and his powerful crime syndicate literally has brand-new life and partners: The CIA. Sosa was expressly requested by the Americans to assist them with helping the Nicaraguan Contra Army stay afloat in the fight against the Sandinista Government. In return, Sosa demands that U.S. Marine Colonel Oliver North allow his organization – La Corporacion Mafia

Cruenza – be allowed to fly fifty jets several times per week into the United States.

While Sosa, his Mafia, the CIA and President Ronald Reagan's National Security Advisor were involved in one of the most blatant and unethical conspiracies in American history, Elvira focuses on her pregnancy... and learns what real power feels like. As she absorbs that feeling, she learns also that she can't outrun demons buried in her past. To deal with them, she writes a book entitled *Dark Flight*.

It was a can of worms best kept closed....

MOB TALES, $16.95 & $5.00 S/H: In 1992, Suge 'The Mobfather' Knight launched Death Row Records with a rumored 1.5-million-dollar investment from then-incarcerated drug kingpin Michael 'Harry O' Harris. Under Suge Knight's leadership, Death Row would go on to boast a roster consisting of some of the greatest names in hip-hop history, such as Dr. Dre, Snoop Dogg, and Tupac Shakur. Suge ultimately generated well over 200 million dollars selling records that detailed life in the streets.

Now, from his prison cell, Suge Knight has partnered up with incarcerated publishing boss Mike Enemigo, and longtime Mob affiliate O.G. Silk, to create Death Row Publishing, and drop a new series, *Mob Tales*, as a platform to shed light on some of the hottest incarcerated street-lit authors in the game today. Each book in this series will be a collection of stories written by those who have lived that of which they write, and who are surely to be among the next generation of street-lit legends.

AOB, $15.00 & $5.00 S/H. Growing up in the Bay Area, Manny Fresh the Best had a front-row seat to some of the coldest players to ever do it. And you already know, A.O.B. is the name of the Game! So, When Manny Fresh slides through Stockton one day and sees Rosa, a stupid-bad Mexican chick with a whole lotta 'talent' behind her walking down the street tryna get some money, he knew immediately what he had to do: Put it In My Pocket!

AOB 2, $15.00 & $5.00 S/H.

AOB 3, $15.00 & $5.00 S/H.

PIMPOLOGY: THE 7 ISMS OF THE GAME, $15.00 & $5.00 S/H: It's been said that if you knew better, you'd do better. So, in the spirit of dropping jewels upon the rare few who truly want to know how to win, this collection of exclusive Game has been compiled. And though a lot of so-called players claim to know how the Pimp Game is supposed to go, none have revealed the real. . . Until now!

JAILHOUSE PUBLISHING FOR MONEY, POWER & FAME: $19.99 & $7.00 S/H: In 2010, after flirting with the idea for two years, Mike Enemigo started writing his first book. In 2014, he officially launched his publishing company, The Cell Block, with the release of five books. Of course, with no mentor(s), how-to guides, or any real resources, he was met with failure after failure as he tried to navigate the treacherous goal of publishing books from his prison cell. However, he was determined to make it. He was determined to figure it out and he refused to quit. In Mike's new book, *Jailhouse Publishing for Money, Power, and Fame*, he breaks down all his jailhouse publishing secrets and strategies, so you can do all he's done, but without the trials and tribulations he's had to go through...

All books are available on thecellblock.net website.

You can also order by sending a money order or institutional check to:

The Cell Block
PO Box 1025
Rancho Cordova, CA 95741

Made in the USA
Middletown, DE
01 June 2025

76387565R00157